Acknowledgements

Big thanks to Edward R. Morris (for editing and German) and Larry Hall, for being great trusted first draft readers, Cari, for putting up with hours of Oi! coming out of the office while I was writing this.

Stand Alone, Dennis Childers, Jessie Keith, and Rat, for actual old school British advice on Oi! to listen to during the writing process (too bad he doesn't read), Big John (because there is a 50% chance he has AF Skinhead hoodie while you read this).

Susan and Anne Lynch, for answering late 80's Chicago Transit Authority questions.

Jeff, Rose, Carl, Cameron and the whole crew at Eraserhead.

To my true friends and family.

BOOKS BY DAVID AGRANOFF

The Vault of Punk Horror
Screams from a Dying World
The Vegan Revolution . . . with Zombies
Hunting the Moon Tribe

BOOT BOYS
OF THE WOLF REICH

DAVID AGRANOFF

deadite
press

deadite
press

DEADITE PRESS
205 NE BRYANT
PORTLAND, OR 97211
www.DEADITEPRESS.com

AN ERASERHEAD PRESS COMPANY
www.ERASERHEADPRESS.com

ISBN: 978-1-62105-140-4

For Jack, Alan, Brendan and Trish

"Treu, Taper, Gehorsam."
—Nazi S.S. motto

"Hard times coming your way . . ."
—The Cro-Mags

"The sun is setting and the day is late,
As we walk over this wasteland of hate.
There's people getting angry in these darkest hours.
There's blood on the streets and the streets are ours . . .
It's your hate on which we feed.
We are the new class. We are the new breed . . ."
—Blitz

PROLOGUE

It happens to all monsters, when you see that look in the eyes of others. It's hatred and fear, mostly, but they know exactly what you are.

The Jew stared at Klaus, as he stood at attention beside the road. The rest of the camp staff, all of them S.S., were getting into line and nervously adjusting lapels and creases on their uniforms.

Klaus, in turn, stared back at the Jew, who stood motionless, seemingly impervious to the biting cold of the frigid Polish winter. When Klaus snapped his fingers, the Jew walked on in a large arc to avoid the camp Commandant.

Commandant Schmidt was a tub of lard who'd managed to avoid active duty in the war (as an aide-de-camp to *der Führer* himself, no less!). Klaus bit his tongue as the Commandant stepped into the light, in that empty S.S. uniform he could not possibly have earned. He was almost popping out of it like an over-packed sausage. The great fat man standing before them was hardly a vision of racial purity.

"*Gruppenführer,*" was all Klaus said. The Commandant nodded. Klaus snapped his outstretched hand in a salute. A dozen arms lifted likewise to salute the Führer. The Commandant just waved them off with a snot-drenched rag, and spoke softly.

"*Was machen sie hier?* What is this about?" Klaus looked confused.

"They asked for you, sir."

Klaus squinted. Before he could think about it, the camp guards were cranking the sirens. He and all his S.S. *offizieren* knew this meant their guest had arrived, but the Jews scurried as if this were an actual air-raid.

Yet one woman stayed, crying and holding something

9

to her chest. Klaus knew her face. She'd worked in the Commandant's office several months ago. He almost remembered her name.

When Commandant Schmidt walked a bit closer, the woman pointed at them, yelling and cursing in frantic Polish, which Klaus could still barely understand. When she held up the bundle in her arms and turned slightly, Klaus hissed in breath. A stillborn, grotesquely underdeveloped baby, with tiny purple feet, and malformed arms that were barely there.

The woman glared daggers at Schmidt, and paused in her flood of profanity to take a breath, screaming briefly in halting German: "*Deinen! Deinen! Ihr ist deinen!*"

He is yours. Klaus' stomach lurched. The Commandant merely snapped his fingers.

Two guards rushed up and grabbed her arms, pulling her away from what he now saw was an unfinished grave. She dropped the child, screaming guttural hatred, barely in words. A group of Jews gathered on the edge of the camp to stare at Klaus and the Commandant.

"Rats, all of them," was Schmidt's only comment. The Jews walked on.

Prisoners were free to walk between the work areas and their crowded quarters. Despite the cold, several dozen were outside, now running back to their bunkhouses. Klaus was used to the sight, having been head of security for almost six months.

He hated this place as much as he supposed the Jews did. The worst part was that he didn't smell them anymore. Their filthy stench had drifted into the background, as had the ash-pit smell from the south end of the camp. The Jews stayed away from that end. He never had to warn them. They were very self-policing about that, in that they simply knew that when prisoners went to that end, they didn't come back. Q.E.D.

Then the camp gates were clanking open. A shiny, brand-new-looking Bayerisch Moteren-Werke Sonderklasse limousine rolled imperiously into the camp on bulletproof tires. The driver was a young S.S. corporal, probably fresh from the choirboy ranks of the *Hitler-Jugend* divisions. He opened the back door, and almost every jaw dropped.

Reinhard Heydrich stepped out of the limo into the cold night, blinking and looking around. There were whispers almost immediately. Himmler's second-in-command of fifteen years hadn't been seen outside Berlin for months. Instantly, the sounds of snapping boot heels and *Sieg Heils* were everywhere.

Commandant Schmidt was the first to step forward, eyes obsequious and voice oleaginous. "Herr Heydrich, *willkomen.* I cannot tell you, sir, what a supreme honor it is to—"

Heydrich didn't even look at Schmidt, who swallowed something in his throat that sounded like his own pride, looking at the ground as Himmler's hatchet-man proceeded past him to stop in front of Klaus, looking him up and down once with no expression on his cold, pale face.

"Herr Schroeder," Heydrich said in a clipped voice, his diction almost Prussian. He let the smile touch his eyes slightly. "What an honor it is to finally meet you in person."

Klaus permitted himself to return the smile. "*Mein herr,* the honor is mine."

The camp siren wailed again. This time, the guards were shouting orders. Machine guns locked into place all around.

"Herr Schroeder, order your men down."

The Commandant whistled. The gate was still open, and a large truck bounced through it into the camp, the Mercedes-Benz logo as prominent as a swastika across its grille. All who were present watched nervously as the driver (who did not look like a non-commissioned officer in the slightest) killed the motor with a heavy sigh of valves.

A full dozen black-clad *Schutzkommando* S.S. leapt from the back of the truck, formed ranks and snapped to attention. Klaus Schroeder was a tall man, nearly two meters in height. As the commandos stood silently before him in formation, he reflected that every hand-picked killer he saw was roughly equal to his height, and likely racial purity.

He also noticed Schmidt shaking in his boots like a pudding. In the Third Reich, transfers of command were often conducted in exactly this fashion. Klaus relaxed quite a bit. This could only bode well for him, to 'line his pockets and do himself homage,' as the barbarian English playwright Shakespeare called it. Not a thing wrong with that. Not to him.

Schmidt was begging now, and his eyes showed it as much as his voice attempted not to. "Herr Heydrich, sir, please . . . If I may . . ."

Again, Reinhard Heydrich never even looked in Schmidt's direction. "Herr Schroeder," he queried, in that calm, icy voice that had probably sent more men to their deaths than Schmidt had ever commanded, "I have the understanding that just last week, we transferred four paratroopers of the United States 101st Airborne into your custody. Is this not so?"

Klaus' head chopped up and down twice. "*Jawohl,* Herr Heydrich. The men from the American Airborne divisions were spies, trying to get close to the camp to photograph the Jews, to document what it is that we do here."

Heydrich's head cocked, eyes glittering like a stoat's. "Does holding them here," he gestured around them with one gloved hand, "Not violate every convention of warfare? Surely the *Führer*'s lessons on tactical economy have not escaped you?"

Klaus Schroeder frowned, and Heydrich mistook the frown for confusion. "They are prisoners of war, no matter how the die is cast," he continued, "And . . .should one escape, as these American rats have been known to do . . . then they have achieved their mission, in the end. Surely you see the sense of this."

Now Klaus' own eyes were glittering. "I considered that possibility," he conceded. "But then the Allies would have to admit that they sent them in the first place. Ah?"

Heydrich barked something that was supposed to be a laugh. Incredibly, he shook Klaus Schroeder's hand. "You have a fine mind," he said in a more conversational tone. "Officer material from the beginning, just as it says in your file. Good man. Pillar of the Reich."

Inwardly, Klaus beamed, though his face betrayed

nothing. "I have been making their acquaintance for the better part of a week," he explained earnestly. "These Americans are hardy. Two of them have broken, the two who clearly barely made it through Ranger training."

Heydrich looked interested. "Have we gleaned any information of value?"

Klaus spat. "I had to use pentothal on the first. The second broke under the d-Lysergic acid diethylamide we have on hand from the Swiss. Still they only talk of home, how their Papas treated them, their girls . . . Nothing of value. Still, they will break if we keep them here long enough. The move is . . ." He stifled the smirk, "Economical. I promise you that we are very close to a breakthrough, and—"

Heydrich held up one hand, cutting him off. "I care nothing for timetables, presently," he replied almost airily. "May I meet with the American prisoners?"

Klaus looked at the dozen commandos, then back at their CO. *What is the game, here?* Yet despite the thought, agreement was the only choice available to him. Without a word more, they proceeded back through the camp, down the long service road in front.

As they walked, Klaus could feel eyes on him. His daily rounds had inured him to the venom and hatred in the eyes of the *Juden*. After a few weeks in camp, that melted away into sorrow and hopelessness at his own situation.

Klaus wondered how it felt to Heydrich, who was normally isolated by command-structure from the reality of the Final Solution. No, the eyes Klaus felt now were those of the stormtroopers standing guard by the truck. *Did Heydrich not trust his security? Were those men sizing him up?*

As they approached the long cinder block bunker where Klaus housed the prisoners, he noticed Heydrich pull out a handkerchief and cover his nose as they walked. Almost idly, Klaus remembered that the smell of the crematorium, was foul and thick at this end of the camp. Those ovens roared for twenty-one hours of each and every day.

Ruminating, Klaus pulled out his heavy ring of keys, unlocked the door and leaned against it. It fell open. His heart dropped as he saw the empty cell.

"*Gruppenführer.*" Heydrich was far too calm. That could mean nothing good.

Klaus stepped back, revealing the empty cell. There was little point in speaking, and he had no interest in begging for his life. Instead, he let his eyes travel to the camp walls, through the lightly-falling snow that swirled in a slight breeze. *There.* The barbed wire was mangled open at one wide point. The Americans had escaped into the woods.

"Herr Schroeder, I suggest you find your prisoners," Heydrich informed him. Klaus could barely blink. He was being given a second chance. "I shall gather my men," he replied stiffly, trying not to stammer.

"No," Heydrich turned to his personal guard. Without a word, the big corn-fed Rheinlander commando handed him a rifle, which Heydrich presented to Klaus. "You must find them alone."

As before, agreement was the only option available.

***

It would have scared most men to death, but tracking humans was Klaus Schroeder's favorite sport. It was a skill that allowed him to rise quickly through the ranks of the S.S. as a younger man. He'd been honored once in Berlin, by the Führer himself, and was now entrusted by Himmler to lead security at one of the most important camps, home to research being done by the greatest scientists in the Fatherland.

Schroeder was able to document his pure Aryan heritage with family records dating back even further than the required year of 1750. Raised in the crushing poverty after the Great War and watching the Führer rebuild their nation, Klaus understood that only Germany could be responsible for the future.

He would return with the heads of the four spies, this night. He would prove his worth to Heydrich, to Himmler; and, of course, to his Führer. Even as the thought took shape, he saw the heavy prints of American Airborne-issue boots (which he'd mercifully allowed the prisoners to retain) leading deeper into the woods.

Fools. They would soon find that the way they took led only to a shallow lake, and a ridge that was nearly impossible to climb. Had they headed north along the edge of the camp, they could have followed the road to the village, and perhaps made it there by dawn.

Klaus could not allow himself to be beaten by these impure American savages, with their loud, grating accents and unthinkable beliefs. He hunkered down and began to run.

After what must have been about an hour, he heard the Yank bastards. They walked at a slow pace.

Like a wolf, he melted into the shadows, listening to them speak.

He understood a little more English than he did Polish, but not by much. There were a few cognates with German, but American English was hopelessly full of slang and colloquialism. They spoke just above a whisper, but it was clear they didn't believe they were being followed. Of course they expected dogs, and a search party.

"I gotta sit," one of them was saying. "Just a minute."

Mallory, their commanding officer, refused to stop. He just kept walking. Bishop, the foul-mouthed half-breed, kept close to Mallory. But the other two soldiers, Thomas and Rosenberg, sat down on a rock. Klaus knew he could make it to their position.

"Mallory, we need water." Thomas practically begged. In the shadows, Klaus thought of Schmidt begging. His lip curled, lupine as his earlier movements had been. Mallory ignored Thomas. Meanwhile, Klaus slung his rifle and detached the bayonet blade.

After he did, he lowered himself quietly to the wet forest floor, and crawled. The snow wasn't sticking yet, but he knew he could be seen easily with it landing on his black uniform. Still he crawled quietly up behind the rock where Rosenberg and Thomas sat. He was close enough to smell them.

Klaus had spent the most time with Thomas, allowing Rosenberg to stare out the cell and watch his already-exhausted

15

Jewish relatives march in chains to the crematorium. That must have been hard. Good. He could tell the Devil about it down in Hell.

Thomas, too, had been so close to breaking. Klaus would enjoy more sessions with these men, but his orders were clear.

It was time. Before his brain even knew what it was doing, Klaus popped up like a vampire from behind the rock and knocked the men's heads together. Rosenberg fell back first, and Klaus' bayonet circumnavigated Rosenberg's neck so fast that his scream drowned in the blood gushing from his throat.

Klaus' right hand snaked out, once again with few orders from his brain, and crushed Thomas' windpipe. He felt the hyoid bone snap, and heard Thomas' gargling scream, much louder than the kike's had been, as he twisted his bayonet in the American's chest.

Mallory and Bishop were coming back down the trail. They stopped when Klaus dropped Thomas before them like a sack of grain. Mallory didn't have a weapon, but dropped into a boxer's stance.

Covered in blood, holding the bayonet high, Klaus waved him forward. "Come on then, Yank," he whispered in a voice as calm as Heydrich's.

Mallory took a step.

Suddenly, the world lit up, as though a full bank of Klieg floodlights had been turned on them. All three men were blinded, covering their eyes, flailing into defensive postures.

Before Klaus could open his own eyes, he heard Mallory gasp. Then he heard them breathing. Panting like dogs. In that white glare, he could almost feel their fetid breath fan his neck, and condense on his face.

He heard Mallory gasp, and was afraid to open his eyes. Just under the spotlights, a pack of wolves surrounded them on all fours, looking ready to spring. The alpha of the pack howled, and then they all began to harmonize, reaching their heads toward the full moon just above the trees.

Klaus wasn't sure he'd ever heard a wolf's howl sound exactly like these. He shook to his core, as Mallory was

16

shaking, dropping a bucket's worth of sweat. Even as he noticed this, the pack was in motion, circling them slowly and gently, stepping lightly around them.

Mallory spun his back to Bishop. Each and every time they stepped towards the wolves, they growled. Then, out of nowhere, they were silent. Sitting, like Shepherd-dogs. Forming ranks, six on a side.

Even the veteran tracker Klaus Schroeder hadn't caught the approach of the man in the cloak and cowl. But Klaus saw the red Thule Society ring on his left index finger, poking out from the wide sleeve of the black cloak like a talon, as he stepped into the circle.

Then he saw the face beneath the cowl. It was a face he'd only ever seen in blurry photographs in communiques from the Intelligence Service. Seeing it here was unnerving, even to a man of his particular sensibilities.

"*Sicherheitsdienstliter* Wilhelm Muller", Mallory whispered. Muller smiled but kept his hands behind his back. The wolves were up again, now, circling faster. Impatient.

"Gruppenführer Schroeder," SD Leiter Muller rasped. "I am honored to be with you on this night."

Klaus was flummoxed. "What is happening, *Mein Herr?*"

Muller took a step forward, smiling at the question as though Klaus were a child in kindergarten. His strange eyes betrayed nothing.

"I have spoken to Wotan, and Thor, and even Loki of the Fire" he answered, without a trace of hyperbole, "I have communed with the Teutonic lord-kings who hacked together this kingdom from nothing." When he grinned, his teeth were sharper than Klaus' senses could support. "Your ancestors speak very highly of you."

Klaus was speechless. Muller steepled his scrimshaw nails as though the two of them were at a briefing, in a warm room, not out here where the stars gave no shelter and the snow no peace.

"Tell me, *Gruppenführer*, are you a mouse … or a wolf?" Muller pulled his hands around his cloak, and held a wolf's hide before him. The hide was large enough to be a fur coat, but it had no arms, merely the flat skin of a Gray wolf.

Muller stepped closer to Klaus. The wolves were now circling fast enough to run. Bishop screamed something incoherent, running toward Muller. One of the wolves launched itself at him and brought him to the ground. It took a moment, and most of the sounds weren't very nice.

Muller stood beside Klaus. "I would stand still, Major Mallory," he croaked in perfect, almost-accentless English. On the ground, Bishop was DOA, face pointed toward the stars, turning the snow pink in a long drag-mark as the wolf half-hauled, half-threw him toward the bodies of his compatriots at Klaus' feet.

Bishop (who'd spit in Klaus' face during the first day of interrogation), was now whimpering and begging. Klaus suddenly forgot his English, or pretended he did, and kicked Bishop's hand away from his trouser cuff. He wasn't surprised to see Muller handing him the hide cloak, which he reached for. Once again, his assassin's hands did the thinking. His brain had very little to do with it.

Muller handed the Wolf-skin to Klaus. It felt hot in his hands. He gave Klaus a reassuring pat on the shoulder. "It is the skin of Ophois, the Egyptian Wolf-God. Many brave Aryan soldiers gave their lives at the temple of Lykoplis to acquire it."

Klaus had no idea if Muller was talking sense. They were well past that point. The SD Leiter's knife-rack smile was strangely paternal. "Go ahead, *mein sohn.* Put it on."

Major Mallory stood there stiffly, trying to look dignified. He didn't. "What is happening here?" he asked with resolve in his voice. When Muller turned to look at him, Mallory backed up a step. The stray wolf returned to the running circle.

"We are celebrating," Muller told him. "You, Major are the main course,"

Muller displayed his palms, and Mallory gasped at the inverted pentagrams that boiled up in red across their pale pink surfaces. Klaus put the wolf-skin over his back, watching avidly.

Then his blood was running white-hot as the Moon, inside him. *Old Father Wotan was calling, calling, calling him to change his skin, and run with Wotan on the Wild Hunt* . . . More immediately, his every joint was screaming like a chicken drumstick being twisted from the bird, but it was good. Felt good. Warm. Change. Skin. Changing.

Changing. When the wolves began to harmonize, he wanted to howl along. The human hand on his shoulder had long nails, the smell . . .

Alpha.

Muller saw Klaus' nose go up, even as the blood ran from Schroeder's gums and his eyes lit newly red. He was beaming.

"Wilkommen, Herr Schroeder. Wilkommen bis in der Wülfreich."

ONE

Chicago: Summer, 1989

"Wearing braces, the Red, White, and Blue,
Doing what he thinks he ought to do,
Used to be a Punk, and a Mod too,
Or is it just a phase he's going through?
He's a clockwork skinhead,
Just a clockwork skinhead . . ."

—The 4-Skins

One day removed from his last day as a sophomore in high school, Paul had slept through most of the six-hour drive north from the only home he'd ever known in Carbondale, Illinois. The tape ran out long after he fell asleep in the back seat. It woke him when the Walkman snapped to STOP.

In the distance, the Chicago skyline came into view. He flipped his tape over. It was a mix tape of New York City hardcore bands; mostly Sick of It All and Agnostic Front loud enough to drown out his parents (who were presently arguing directions. Again.). He'd already pushed the Play button when his Mom turned to look at him.

"Good," she observed. "You're awake."

"Nah," Paul shook his head and closed his eyes. His mother reached back and pulled the headphones off her son's head.

"This is a big deal, Paulie. We should do this as family. Daniel, tell your son what's what."

Paul shut off his Walkman. "What's wrong with music?"

"*Music* is fine. I don't know what you call *that*. Margie, don't forget to tell me where we turn next."

20

Daniel (also known as Dad) couldn't resist a chance to jab his son about his music. Paul wasn't having it.

"Funny, because I know Grandma loved all your hippie crap."

His Mom clearly didn't like that. 'Grandma' was still pretty close to a dirty word in their family. Paul's Grandma had gradually chilled out on wanting, despite her disapproval of the marriage, to be in her grandson's life.

Mom was practically thrown out of the family when she got serious about a boy who wasn't Jewish. When she came home with an engagement ring from a Black radical she knew from campus, no one wanted to admit color had anything to do with it. But it was hard to deny.

Paul didn't mind his parents too much. To him, they were sold-out late Sixties radicals who raised hell at the university of Chicago as student organizers. They were now set to return there, but History and Sociology profs, respectively.

"This is music!" His Dad announced, popping a tape into the station wagon's stereo and pretending to rock out as Jimi Hendrix launched into "All Along the Watchtower."

Mom laughed. Paul just shook his freshly-shaven, side-burned head. "This is hippie hair-farmer *shit . . .*"

***

And on it went. Paul laced up his combat boots as they pulled into the driveway. The house was huge, bigger than their old one, but crammed in between two other fancy-looking houses.

He reached behind him and grabbed his black bomber jacket, even though the temperature was in the seventies. Meditatively rubbing his freshly-shaven head, he stepped out of the car and looked around, letting his thick red suspenders fall to his side.

Paul was as decked out in skinhead uniform as he could be. He had to let the neighborhood know right away there was a new Skin in town.

He had his reasons. In all actuality, Hyde Park was as

21

nice a neighborhood as the South Side could boast. It was walking distance to campus. There were only a few streets too dangerous to walk on.

Paul would never admit it, but he was nervous. He'd never really been to the big city except museums, and the Sears Tower with Grandma and Grandpa. Paul was a college-town skater who learned about Punk from articles he read in THRASHER magazine, in a town whose only punks or Punk bands were kids going to college at Southern Illinois University.

He first saw a skinhead during a Cro-Mags video on "The Headbangers' Ball." As soon as he saw the tough-looking baldhead, the mohawk he'd worked so hard to grow out felt stupid, like a waste of time and energy. So he shaved his head, unaware of any other aspects of Skinhead fashion. He found an article in *Metal* magazine about a band called Agnostic Front. They had a few skinheads in the band, and Paul modeled his look after them. So far, that worked.

"Little hot for the jacket?" Dad asked, opening the back of the station wagon. Paul just shook his head and grabbed a box of his stuff. "Where's my room?"

"Bedrooms are on the third floor," Mom told him, opening the front door.

Paul walked in and felt a little relief at seeing their old furniture already set up. Dad had been here a week ago, with a floor plan from Mom. She was already launching into Dad about everything being wrong by the time Paul walked into his room.

His old bed, CD player, and skateboard (which he hadn't been on since he was at least fourteen years old) waited for him. He put his box down and sat on the bed. His Dad had put the wrong-sized sheets on it, and the blanket almost slid off.

Slowly he unlaced his combat boots that he bought at the Carbondale Army-Navy surplus store. They were good boots, and they did the trick in Carbondale. But suddenly he felt like a poser. Skinheads wore Doc Marten boots, period.

The soft-soled boots were to work boots what Lamborghinis are to sports cars. He was always going to feel like a poser until he could get himself a pair of Docs. Close to a hundred bucks a pair imported, you could only find them in a few stores in the country.

Paul pulled out a slip of paper, months old, written by a Chicago punk kid at a party in Carbondale: *The Alley. Just off Belmont. Docs!* He put the paper on his night stand and pulled out his wallet. He didn't need to count it. Fifty-five measly bucks.

His door opened, and Mom walked in with a handful of towels. Paul stuffed his wallet away. She opened his drawer and pushed the towels in, looking at him. Clearly, she saw he was upset. "You all right?"

Mom sat on the bed next to him. Paul nodded. His mother saw through it. She wasn't sure what it could be, as no one wanted this move more than Paul. Then she saw the slip of paper on the nightstand.

"Ahhh, the boots."

He looked wounded. "Ma, they're not just boots."

"I know, the doctor boots . . ."

Paul rolled his eyes, jokingly pushing on his mother to get out. The last thing he wanted was her to give him another *'What's wrong with* these *boots?'* speech about his clunky Army boots. But that wasn't what she asked.

"How did you do saving?"

He sighed. "I need another fifty bucks." Mom laughed. Paul shook his head.

"Not funny."

"Well, your birthday is in a month." She stood up. "Save your money and we'll get the rest."

"A month?" Paul sounded whiny. It would have sounded even worse if he said what he was thinking. *I can't meet all the Chicago Skins with these stupid boots.*

Despite the obvious unspoken anguish on her son's face, Margie Jackson smiled. "It's that important to you?" Paul didn't have to say anything.

"How about you give me what you have, we'll go to see a Cubs game and pick up the boots on the way?"

Paul couldn't think of anything more awful than his

23

mother going with him to pick out the docs and putting them on her credit card. "Can't you just front me the money until my birthday?" he countered, still trying mightily not to whine.

Mom sighed deeply. "Okay, but this comes out of your birthday cash."

Paul sighed, too, in a different tone. Relief. "Totally." Margie Jackson frowned, thinking of something. "I can't go with you?"

Now it was a smile he was trying to hide. "No way, Mom."

TWO

"For us, who?
Kids of the 80's,
We don't go to school.
We've given up.
Find a crime.
Just make one up . . ."

—Infa-Riot

It took Sonny a train and two buses, but he arrived at his new home on the west side of Chicago. It was sometimes called a suburb, or a neighborhood of Chicago, depending on who you asked. To Sonny, Blue Island looked like a town that time forgot.

All the signs and storefronts hadn't changed since the Seventies. The A & W drive-in restaurant was still open. It was a far cry from his hometown, even though only thirty or forty miles separated the two.

The bus stopped less than a block from Mansford Auto Parts. Sonny slung his large green Army duffel-bag and stepped off.

Eighteen years and one day old, he promised his mother he'd stay at home until he graduated high school. He played the game, took the tests. Even when he thought a lot of what they taught was bullshit, he answered the questions he was supposed to and technically graduated. He wasn't going to be there for the cap-and-gown crap. His mother already cried about that. His father lectured him. He didn't have to listen anymore.

Sonny checked himself in the reflection of the window at the front of the store. One hundred percent American

Skinhead. Walked into the store, he noticed that Tom Mansford, the owner, was busy discussing car batteries with some customer. He wore the store uniform, which Sonny quickly realized was nearly the same as a skinhead uniform: Shaved head, thin white braces(super-thin suspenders, hanging loose), and clean jeans rolled up over ten-hole Oxblood Doc Martens laced with white laces. The only different part was the auto parts store T-shirt.

Tom waved at Sonny, but kept talking to his customer. A young Skinhead sat behind the counter.

"You must be Sonny, the new kid?"Sonny nodded.

"I'm Smithy. Let me introduce you to the crew."

Smithy lead Sonny through a door into a warehouse-style back room that smelled like tires. Not surprisingly, it was filled with tires. Sonny smiled when he saw the back wall: Nazi flags, Confederate stars-and-bars, and flyers for every gathering of White Power groups around the country. Under the flag was a TV hooked up to a Nintendo, and a couch. A group of skins sat on the couch and in the chairs around the TV.

"Tom said you'd be staying here at the shop for awhile. Hope you like the smell of Goodyears."

They both laughed. Smithy whistled. "Hey, ladies and gents, let me introduce you to Sonny, our new recruit from all the way up in Deerfield."

Everyone laughed at the mention of his far-north rich suburb. He knew he'd get hazed about the 'rich' part, not to mention how close it was to Jew towns like Northbrook. The guys stood up to greet him first.

Sonny was a big guy, but the first guy to walk up on him was a monster, with big mutton-chop sideburns that were almost a beard.The guy pushed his girlfriend out of the way. "I'm John, but the boys call me Chops. This here is my bird, Dana."

Dana was your typical Skinhead girl: big-framed, hair shaved into a Chelsea (short bangs but the rest of the head shaved with a number-2 guard on the clippers). Dana waved, but sat back down.

"I'm Ace," A second overweight skin stepped forward. Ace was grossly out of shape. His girth poked from his t-shirt, which had a picture of Luke Skywalker on it, and read 'I STILL WOULD HAVE NAILED LEIA.'

Ace likewise introduced his skinbird Rachel, who shook his hand. Sonny laughed to himself, thinking that she had a stronger grip than his father did. Ace offered him a seat. Chops walked over to the small fridge in the corner.

"You want a soda? I'd offer you a beer, but drinking at lunch time is for niggers." Everyone laughed.

"Yeah, I'll take a Coke."

Chops threw him a can. "So, White Power in Deerfield, huh?"

"Yeah, I've been a Skin for couple years, you know, but . . ."

"For real," Ace looked surprised.

"I ain't seen you around," said Dana.

Sonny cleared his throat. He didn't really want to tell them that he was a Skinhead for a year before becoming racially aware. He didn't consider himself political, before. The deeper truth was one he couldn't admit to. Then he thought of something.

"It's my parents, and shit. They were control freaks."

No one said anything, That made Sonny uncomfortable. *Keep talking.*

"Nigger lovers. My dad runs some fuckin' bank that gives all kinda loans to niggers on the southside. He's constantly dealing with them being deadbeats, owing him money. He didn't like me being a skin, so I didn't get out much. I finished school, turned eighteen and Tom said I could have a job."

"Fuck 'em," said Chops "Ain't none of our parents understand. Tom's the only dad we need." At that, everyone who wasn't playing the video game raised their cups.

"Be careful with that school stuff, man." Smithy said as he walked back to the store front. "Zionist bullshit."

Sonny looked around the room. His parents fought with him when he put up his Nazi flag, or bought the Confederate flag belt-buckle. Here, he was free to think what he wanted, what he knew to be true. Sonny relaxed in the chair.

27

"Welcome to the family, Sonny," Chops said as he passed Ace the video game controller. Chops looked down at Sonny's Docs. The old Oxblood boots were faded and scuffed up.

"Better get those polished up before your shift tomorrow," Chops said almost paternally.

"Yeah. I was going to take the bus down to the Alley this afternoon and get some polish."

Chops and Dana shared a look. Chops cleared his throat. "I got some polish back at the house. I'll hook you up."

Sonny shook his bald head. "I should have my own."

Chops nervously scratched his leg. "You been to Belmont lately?" Sonny shook his head again.

"What he means to say is we ain't welcome." Rachel piped in.

"Fuckin' Sharps," Ace added bitterly taping away at his video game.

"We scared of them?" Sonny asked right-out.

"Nah, man. Who wants to go there?" Chops said, but his face got a little red. "All them dirty punks hangin' out a couple blocks from Faggot Town."

Maybe this was a way Sonny could prove himself quickly. "I'm not afraid of some fuckin' Sharps."

Ace paused his video. "Sonny, you got balls, man."

"Yeah, and my own polish . . ."

THREE

"I couldn't believe it . . .
She looked at me and smiled.
I know that smile's for me . . .
She wore braces and blue jeans
She was my Skinhead girl
She was my Skinhead girl . . ."

—Symarip

The El station where Paul caught the train by his new house was up above a street he was advised by his father not to be on after dark. Dad handed him a quarter and told him to call home when he got back to the station. Then he'd drive the six blocks to pick him up.

Paul had to transfer trains underground when he got downtown. But by the time he got to Belmont, the train had gone back up above the street. All he knew was that Belmont was a street not far from Wrigley Field, where the Cubs played . . . and that it was the street where all the Punks and Skins hung out when there were no shows to go to.

He saw a punk couple on the train getting off at the Belmont stop, and walked slowly behind them. The guy had a leather jacket with a Dead Kennedys logo, and his multi-colored mohawk stuck sharply in the air like a buzzsaw. When he hit the street across the way, Paul saw a group of skinheads walking together. He felt excited and nervous. He wanted to say hello but also felt dorky, not sure what to say.

The only other skinhead he'd met was a guy named Joe, who lived in a small town near Carbondale called Murphysboro. Not long after Joe became a Skinhead, he moved to St.Louis. The one time Paul met Joe, he gave Paul advice, telling him to put an American flag on his flight jacket, over the pen holder on his arm. They never talked again after that.

Maybe this time he'd just get his boots and go home. Next time, he'd introduce himself. Paul crossed the street, and a car honked at him.

The streets were filled with cars, and the sidewalks were crowded. Just before he got to a major street going the other direction he saw a sign on the corner of the Alley, reading: 'The Alley, this way.' The sign even had a Doc Marten logo.

Paul smiled and walked down the Alley to the store. Inside they were playing some kind of industrial dance music, and a guy behind the counter bopped his spikey hair up and down to the beat. There were racks and racks of t-shirts for Punk bands that he would have killed to have back home. Shirts he had to order out of catalogs he found in the back of THRASHER, or the Burning Airlines Catalogue.

He walked around the maze of shirts toward the boots and his jaw dropped when he saw an entire wall of Doc Martens. Black, maroon, purple and green. Three-hole shoe style, eight-hole short boots, ten hole boots and the super tall sixteen and twenty hole boots.

"Pretty amazing, eh," said a young female voice beside him. Paul snapped back into reality, and saw a real live Skinhead girl standing between him and the black-ten holed Docs he dreamed about for a year.

He looked at her. She was super-cute: his height, athletic, wearing a stretched tight small Fred Perry tennis shirt, a short flowing plaid skirt and black leggings. Her head was shaved into a Chelsea with dyed blond bangs. She smiled through full lips. A small birthmark dotted her left dimple, only adding charm to her smile. Paul immediately broke out in a sweat.

"Uh—"

She put out her hand. "I'm Tracy, I don't think we've met."

"Uh, yeah. I'm Paul. I just moved here."

"From?" Her smile tripled its wattage.

He had to skin up sometime. "Carbondale," he admitted.

"That explains the Army boots," Tracy looked

commiseratingly at his embarrassment and waved it off. "My parents want me to go to college down there. There a lot of skins down there?"

Paul didn't know what to say. She was beautiful. Part of him felt like running.

"No, just me. Well I live here now."

Tracy smiled warmly. "This your first pair of Docs?"

Paul nodded. Tracy walked over to a pair of maroon boots, thumping the steel toe-caps with one knuckle. "I think a pair of ten hole Ox-bloods would look pretty hot."

Paul forgot all about the black boots. "Funny, that's exactly what I was looking for."

Tracy nodded to a woman in a Alley T-shirt, who went to get the boots. Paul sat down and started to unlace his army boots. Tracy grabbed his suspenders.

"These things are thick as rulers."

Paul must have looked confused.

"What color is your bomber?"

He knew she meant his jacket. "Black."

Tracy walked over to a nearby rack and returned with a red thin stretchy things on clips. "You need a pair of braces. Skinheads dress in Docs and braces, not shitkickers and grandpa's suspenders."

Paul sighed. Tracy took his hand. Hers was soft and smooth. He almost freaked out.

"Hey I'm from a town way up north in the suburbs. I get it, you don't know these things. It's okay. I'm not judging. I just want to help . . ."

Paul smiled when he put his foot in the boot. It just felt nice right away. He looped the laces in.

"Oh, no. let me show you."

Paul looked at her eight-hole black Docs and the woman working the store's three-hole shoes. They were laced straight across, like the rungs of a ladder. "Docs will last longer if you ladder-lace them. I'll show you."

Tracy reached over Paul and showed him how to lace his Docs. He bought them and fell in love with Tracy at the same moment.

31

***

Paul stepped out into the alley with his brand-spanking-new Docs and braces. He felt a hundred feet tall. Tracy waited in the alley, one foot up on the wall.

"Oh yeah, Skinhead!"

Paul smiled. He didn't even keep the old boots. He probably wasn't the first skinhead to try and stuff old combat boots into the trash can at the Alley. Tracy handed him a piece of paper. It was her phone number, and she kissed the page with fresh lipstick. "Had to give that to you before you met the other girls."

Paul laughed. He'd only met her a half an hour ago. "I don't want any other numbers."

Tracy smiled. "Good. Lets go meet the crew."

She took his arm, leading him out to Belmont and around the corner to the Dunkin Donuts parking lot. "It gets more hoppin' at night but this is where the crew hangs."

There was only one car parked in the parking lot. It looked like a park. A few punk rockers, including the couple Paul saw on the train, stood around. The Skins he saw walking down the street sat on the curb. Four guys and two women, dressed in full Skinhead gear.

Hanging out with other skinheads was fantasy a few days ago. Here he was, for the first time, with a real live crew. "Hey, everybody we got a new Skin who just moved into town," Tracy said and took Paul down the line.

Everyone was friendly and excited to meet a young new Skinhead. And Paul was much younger than these guys. Tracy introduced Smiley, the only younger skin, first. He had a giant smile and couldn't have been more than twelve years old.

Next to him was a guy Tracy called Rooster. He was from a Northern Indiana crew called NISH, wore a porkpie hat and had a beer wrapped in a paper bag. His girlfriend hung on his arm, but she looked just as tough as him. She introduced herself as Cherry. According to Tracy, they spent most of their time here in the city.

There was a black Skin as big as tree named Marcus,and his girlfriend Shawna. They were Northside boot-boys. Marcus was the eldest skin in Chicago,even hung out with Rude Boys in England during the late 70's two-tone revival. Paul thought Marcus was going to break his hand when they shook.

"Welcome to Chicago, little man."

Paul laughed. He wasn't tiny for his age. Either way, he needed to start working out harder.

Last, Tracy introduced Noah, who was a big guy with a hook nose. Marcus laughed and shook his head. "He ain't Noah, we call him Mossad—the Nazi hunter."

Marcus and Noah slapped hands and laughed. Tracy smiled, and watched Paul looking at his watch.

"Don't tell me you gotta get home?"

Paul didn't know what to say. Dinner with his folks. It all seemed so childish. He just nodded.

"Too bad. It gets pretty fun here after dark. We get some drinks going back in the alley, all the frats get drunk and want to fight on their way out of the Cubby Bear. It's wild."

"Some other time."

Tracy nodded. Everyone shouted to Paul to come back soon. Rooster held up his bottle.

"Can I walk you to the El?" Tracy asked.

"I'd love that."

"Maybe you'll ask me out on a date before we get there."

FOUR

"We've been warned of rivers of blood.
See the trickle before the flood.
Pretend nothing happened, make no fuss.
One law for them,
One for us . . ."

—The 4-Skins

He didn't wear Skinhead gear. He put on his Sox hat and thin zip-up hoodie. He almost put on gym shoes, but then decided that would make him look like too much like a Straight-Edge kid. He couldn't bring himself to not wear his Docs. (Smithy'd joked about him going undercover, and sung the Murphy's Law song "Secret Agent S.K.I.N." as he got dressed and walked out to the bus.)

As the train pulled into the Belmont station, memories flooded back. The first year he was a Skinhead, he loved coming down here. Drinking in the drinking-alley with the boys. Going to hardcore shows, moshing and fighting the drunk frat guys. It was a blast.

Everyone knew what he became, so he'd avoided Belmont. But Smithy said Marcus declared Belmont "Bonehead free." (Marcus had always called white power skins Boneheads, after the SS skull logo, in the British vernacular and the American.)

Sonny got in the turnstile and started to spin with it. On the other side was a baldhead, a young guy in boots and braces. Their eyes met briefly, and then Sonny was out on the street, and the other skin was on his way to his train. Sonny's heart almost stopped. Tracy stood there lighting a cigarette. She looked great in her Fred Perry and skirt.

"Trace."

She almost jumped out of her skin. Her eyes got wide before she looked around in each direction. No one they knew were standing close by.

"Jesus, Sonny. You scared the shit out of me."

"New look for you," he observed. "New four years. You wear it better than Punk. Or cheerleading. Your Mom flipped out on me when you shaved your head. Do you remember that?"

Tracy looked at his outfit. "Did you join Youth of Today, or something?"

Sonny smiled. "Nah, I'm still a skin." He pounded his fist on his chest. Tracy took a long drag before retorting.

"No, dude, you're still a bonehead, is what you are."

Sonny shook his head, moving to walk past her. "Why, aren't you just Queen SHARP."

Tracy put her hand on his arm, stopping him cold. He looked at her hand, feeling just a little weak in the knees. He missed her, and hadn't seen her since last summer.

"Don't go there, Sonny. Marcus ain't gonna talk old times. A Bonehead from Blue Island beat up an Ethiopian guy who ran a fruit stand over by Wrigley. Ever since then cops have been treatin' us like shit. Like all Skins are racist."

Sonny was thinking 'Maybe they should be,' but thought better of it. "Marcus thinks he's the fucking mayor of Belmont now."

Tracy shook her head. "I knew you were angry about us, but . . ."

Sonny shook his head and walked past her, he turned to point. "Shut your fucking mouth!"

Sonny'd never talked to Tracy like that. The look of surprise and fear on her face pissed him off. It reminded him how much he had let her walk over him when their relationship ended. He couldn't believe she thought his views were about her.

"Marcus is an uppity nigger, I'll grant you that, but he ain't my boss."

Tracy absently let her cigarette burn as she stared on in disbelief. A couple who were walking by stopped to watch.

The man was black. He'd stopped out of concern for Tracy. She looked at the couple.

"You really have changed." Tracy paused. "What you said about Marcus. That's a ugly thing to say, Sonny."

"I'm walking to the alley to get some fucking boot polish, and anyone gets in my way . . ."

Sonny shook his head. The man watching stepped closer. His girlfriend pulled at his arm. Sonny just left.

"Don't say I didn't warn you!" Tracy yelled as Sonny crossed in front of traffic, to a chorus of horns and cabbies shouting.

FIVE

Argentina

"Gotta keep on running – with nowhere to go"

—Crux

The old wolf stretched his bones after a long day of work, and thought about the walk home.

While about his daily toil, he looked forward to the deli the whole time. It was demeaning work he did. He believed that about this was as far as a man could fall in his life, to spend a good portion of the day (as a plumber at the Water & Sanitation plant in town), literally knee-deep in half-processed human shit. This was a not-so-subtle metaphor. After getting off work, it took twenty minutes of scrubbing to not smell shit on his fingers.

Even more than his home, the deli was a sanctuary where he could meet old friends and be himself.

The bell rang as he opened the door, and the smell of toasting bread greeted him. He stopped in there every night for a newspaper.

The deli was the only place in this neighborhood that carried German papers. When the right people were here and the locals were elsewhere, he could speak his native tongue, feel free, play chess with his old buddies, and discuss the world that could have been. Every Tuesday, he got sandwich meat here and on a good night he might see an old friend.

The old man stepped up to the counter. Only one other man sat at the table, coffee cup and newspaper held over his face.

"Good evening, Ricardo," Peron, the deli owner said in

37

Spanish. The old man tightened up and his heart beat faster. Speaking Spanish was normal. Even for this traditional Italian man who immigrated here long before Mussolini fell. The real question was why did he make a point to call him Ricardo.

It was the name on his Argentinian citizenship, but why did he say that name? Peron knew his real name, knew all about him. The old man trusted him with his life, but since the day he arrived in Argentina he had no choice.

The old man locked eyes with the deli owner. The fear and disbelief felt solid between them. The old man tensed up as he heard the newspaper folding behind him. *Forget the German paper,* thought the old man and he spoke in Spanish.

"I'll take two pounds of salami and the Buenos Aires paper."

The chair slid across the floor behind him. The man stood up. The old man could smell his excitement and fear.

"Why not the German paper, Herr Schroeder?"

The old man cursed inside, but didn't turn around. He just stared at the deli owner.

"The salami, please."

Peron didn't move. The old man assumed that their was a gun at his back.

"The building is surrounded," The Jew paused "My name is Herman Stern. My mother, my brother and my father died at Auschwitz-Birkenau."

The old man felt an invisible weight on his shoulders. It wasn't guilt. Oh, he'd sat in this very deli and listened to old friends blather on about the guilt they felt. He never felt it, not one second of remorse. The weight he felt was shame.

They had failed their Fuhrer. A proud tradition of Aryan warriors, an army of master race warriors, had fought and died. They came so close, 'and having greatly failed, more greatly dared,' as the Poet said.

Now their army and their Fuhrer were destroyed. History was again mangled and dominated by the rats who eat away at humanity's core.

Now some Jew had a pistol on his back, and expected

Klaus Schroeder to grovel and beg to be forgiven. Klaus turned to face him.

This Herman Stern was short, slightly portly, with a scruffy beard and frightened rabbit eyes. He also held a small, handy-looking Beretta .9mm level at his chest.

"You don't honestly expect me to say I'm sorry? Weep for your family."

The Jew looked nervously around. He shook his head."I don't expect humanity from a monster like you."

Klaus laughed. "Good. That's good. You have no idea what kind of monster I really am . . ."

***

The Mossad agents sat in several cars parked around the building. They knew for almost a year that the deli was an Odessa meeting spot. Old SS operatives didn't always get packages but they met here for coffee, and sandwiches. The Argentine government had been embarrassed by Nazi captures before, so they did everything they could to block their efforts to find Klaus Schroeder. They insisted that he was a citizen born in the country and a faithful employee of the public works.

Agent Stern knew better, which was why Simon let him make the arrest. They waited, counting off the seconds since Schroeder walked into the deli. Simon tried not to look at his watch when he heard a shot fired inside.

Ten Mossad agents in five different cars all jumped out, and quickly went into action. Simon was closest to the door. The bell rang over the sound of agonized screams. Agent Stern was trying to stand, but sliding on a blood-splattered floor.

He dropped his gun, trying to hold in his shredded intestines. Stern's face was marked by long scratches that bled into his mouth causing him to gurgle as he screamed in pain.

The deli owner screamed too, and wailing and overcome with terror behind the counter. Simon looked. The owner didn't look harmed. He simply covered his eyes, and screamed. Outside a wolf howled so loudly it could have been nothing else, not a dog or a bird of any kind or even a *coyotito*.

A wolf in Buenos Aries? Simon ran through the back room toward an open door. The dusk had grown darker just in the last few moments.

Simon almost missed it. In the corner of his eye, a wolf sped out of the alley, past two stunned agents.

"Shoot it, goddamn it!" Simon yelled at them.

It was too late, The wolf had left them in the dust. And left its bloody pawprints coming out of the store in a long trail similarly crimson, which Simon only saw as he bent to pick up his radio.

An agent walked into the alley holding Schroeder's shredded work overalls. Doctor Stein, the Nazi hunter from the Weisenthal Center, came through the back door with a hankerchief over his mouth and nose.

"Where is he? Schroeder?"

Simon didn't have a clue how to answer that.

SIX

"It was the day at school
When we learned the Golden Rule
The teacher, she taught us,
So we could never be a fool.
And she Skank, and she Skank,
And she Skank into a Rastaman.
Skanking Matilda, Matilda with you . . ."

—The Silvertones

Paul had learned by now that Belmont was a street on the north side, pretty close to Wrigley field. There was a dance club called Medusa's that played mostly house and industrial. A few skinheads worked security over there. They also hosted hardcore shows from time to time.

Down the street was The Alley. Back deep into the alley behind the Alley was a little cave between apartment buildings, under an El track. This was the Drinking Alley, where skins of all ages got their drinks, since it was impossible at their main hangout around the corner at the infamous Punkin' Donuts.

11:00 curfew was a bummer, but Tracy had said yes to a date that included dinner before hangin' out with the crew. By the time he'd meet her at Muskies (a Fifties-style diner on the corner of Belmont and Sheffield) a cool enough breeze would be coming off Lake Michigan for him to wear his bomber jacket.

Mom asked Paul why he wasn't dressing up, and lots of questions about Tracy. Outside of where she was from and her status as a skinhead he responded to with several 'I don't know yet's.'

Far from the tough-guy image skinheads often project,

41

Paul cranked up the first Specials album and skanked around the room, too excited to contain himself. He didn't calm down for the entire train ride across town.

It got even worse when he walked out of the turnstile on to Belmont. She was dressed up in a rude-girl outfit and topped off with a flower pinned above her ears to her Chelsea. The flower perfectly matched her lipstick.

"Damn! Girl! You look . . ."

Tracy smiled. "You're pretty handsome yourself."

Paul gave his best *aww-shucks* look back. "So, fries and a milkshake?"

But Paul barely touched his fries. He couldn't stop talking. They talked about his hometown. She talked about hers, and then transitioned into talking about the Chicago skin scene. Paul loved every second.

But when she so much as mentioned the alley behind the Alley, Tracy looked at her watch.

"Get the check. Lets go!" Paul looked at his own watch, and was properly amazed at how much time had gone by. Amazed, bemused . . .but not surprised.

Tracy held his arm as they walked down toward the spinning Dunkin' Donuts sign. Cars were jammed at each corner bumper-to-bumper, trying to get to and from the crazy night life of Chicago's North side. When they turned the corner Paul couldn't believe his eyes.

His hometown didn't have any skinheads. It didn't even have this many punk rockers, or at least he didn't think so. The parking lot was jammed. The manager stood on the curb, in an argument with two cops who couldn't get the crowd to move.

This debate happened almost nightly. The bodies were too thick, and when a car wanted to pull in they honked. Maybe just maybe people would move.

A car was parked near a Dumpster at the edge of the parking lot. The car was covered in stickers for Oi! and Ska bands. All the doors were open, and the car stereo blasted the song "Jack The Lad" by The 4-Skins. Two skins, a big red-faced lad and a byrd with a Chelsea of similar hue, sat on the

42

trunk smoking. Tracy leaned over to tell Paul about everyone.

"So, Rooster," who was sitting on the trunk smoking, "Worked as a tattoo artist, and recently moved up from Chesterton. If you don't know where that is, it's a little town outside of Gary, Indiana. Cherry always lived in Chicago, and she's been Skin longer than Rooster."

"For real? Why they call him Rooster?" Paul wasn't looking away from her eyes.

"Ha! They call him Rooster because he still had mohawk the first time he hooked up with Cherry. A super tall one." Her words were almost drowned out by both Shawna and her Skin, big Marcus, both howling Cockney exclamations of delight as the mix-tape faded into Madness' "Night Boat To Cairo."

Tracy pointed at them.

"Shawna's Dad was a Jamaican immigrant to London in the Sixties, and an original Skinhead. Spirit of 1969, and all that. Everybody thinks she's just a black Chicago kid, but the south side she grew up on was the south end of London. She married Marcus so he could stay in England." Tracy smiled "But they were in love and came back a few years ago when Marcus inherited a house from his grandmother."

Paul sounded astonished. "Her Dad was an original skin?"

"Yep, she's this scene's direct connection to the factory workers in 'Sixties London who started the whole Skinhead thing. Her father isn't really into it these days, but Shawna kept the tradition alive."

Across the parking lot a few people danced. Several groups of people talked. A few kids were skateboarding in one section, doing Ollies and grinding curbs. That set off the already angry manager. Again.

Paul stared wide-eyed at the scene. It was like nothing he had ever seen. They walked close to the car. Little twelve-year old Smiley sat next to a Skinhead girl old enough to be his mother (maybe she was, Paul thought) The woman smiled at them. "This your new man, Trace?"

Tracy smiled at Paul and looked back at the woman. "I hope so. Is this yours?" Tracy pointed at Smiley. The little man smiled."She hopes so." Everyone laughed.

Marcus stepped up and patted Paul on the shoulder."Hey. The cops are going to kick us out. We're meeting Mossad in the alley for some beers. You have time for a beer?"

Tracy looked at Paul. He looked at his watch. He had two hours before he had to catch the El back to Hyde Park. He was going to love every second of it.

"Hell, yeah!"

***

Sonny breathed a deep sigh of relief as Tom flipped the store sign back to CLOSED. Closing up for his first Friday with the boss sounded all right at first, but they were getting to the party late. Still, he was glad for the chance to get to know Tom.

The word around the store was that Tom became a State Trooper right out of 'Nam. He didn't talk about what happened, but all kinds of legends went around the store. Maybe he used excessive force on a black man who raped a white girl. Maybe he shot a hair-farmer war protester, or maybe he was just outed for being a ol'timey Klansman like his Papa.

Tom was a twice-elected Grand Wizard of the Ku Klux Klan of Illinois. Long before the National Front and Skrewdriver took on the skinhead imagine, he was a real live race-warrior. Early to embrace the Skinheads when most Klansmen saw them as clowns, Tom was thus seen nationally as an innovator, whose methods were 'borrowed' by the Posse Comitatus and the White Aryan Resistance further West. Tom had allied his own recruits with the Northern Hammerskins.

When kids from around the area got fed up with their multi-cultural surroundings, when their parents rejected them for opening their eyes, Tom was there for them. When they got back to his house, it was only four blocks, but they still drove. Things were already hopping.

You could hear Skrewdriver blasting from the house. Thudding could be felt in the driveway. The house was separated by an abandoned house to the right, and a freeway off ramp lifted above them on the left. So they could get as loud as they felt like.

Having slept on the floor or the couch at the store for the last few days, it was Sonny's first time at the house. Tom led him around the house to the backyard. A fire was burning away in the firepit. Smithy was at the grill managing hamburgers and hot dogs. Murphy, Tom's only friend his age, sat on a easy chair he'd broken dragging into the yard.

Sonny walked towards a trash can filled with ice and Budweiser. On his way, he heard Billy talking to two very young-looking blond girls who were both nursing beers. He was a little tipsy, but managing to hold the Zionist control of the media.

As Sonny cracked open his beer one of the girls said "No way," in Valley-girl voice. Sonny looked across the yard at Tom, and held up his beer in salute. Tom laughed. His enormous belly shook before he Sieg-Heiled back at him.

This was the first time in awhile that Sonny felt comfortable socially. When he grew up he was the last kid picked for sports and always picked on. Until he discovered Punk Rock.

His older brother went through a Punk phase that never got deeper than The Clash and the Sex Pistols. He passed the records on to Sonny, and when Little Brother went to high school with spiked hair, things changed.

They still made fun of him, but the cool kids were to afraid to beat up on him. When he shaved his head, everyone shut up for good. Everyone at school except Tracy was afraid of him.

Tracy had a Punk cousin, and a serious need to piss off her mother. Tracy's mother hated Sonny as much as a parent could. After Sonny met the parents for the first time Tracy's mom told her that Sonny was filled with rage. If he was being honest with himself, he would have admitted she was right. *Why shouldn't he be angry?*

Sonny took a deep swig. Ace almost made him choke by patting him on the back. "Hey, it's Undercover Skin." Billy

45

whistled the 'Mission Impossible' theme for a moment, then went back to explaining the problem of race-mixing to the twelve-year-old girls.

Back up on the porch, three drunk Skins sang along to the Skrewdriver song 'Back with a Bang.' Ace stumbled a bit. His face was red. He was loaded already, trying to straighten his shirt that read 'Free Mustache Rides' over his belly.

"So you went up to Belmont."

Sonny had tried to put that day out of his mind. Smithy came up to them with a half-eaten burger.

"Yeah, so you see any SHARPs up there?"

Sonny took a swing and wiped his mouth. "My stupid bitch ex-girlfriend."

"Does she fuck niggers?" Ace asked, almost falling over.

"What the fuck kinda question is that?" Smithy hit him in the arm. Inwardly, Sonny remembered Tracy telling him once that she thought Marcus was hot. An image of his black hand on her skin made him shudder.

"Man those SHARP girls will fuck anything" Ace didn't let it go. "Niggers, spics. They love fucking Jews. Might think their dicks are as big as their noses."

"What did your old lady say to you?" Smithy asked. Sonny thought about saying nothing. He should have, but he was still pissed."She said this fucked-up shit about not coming around anymore, that Marcus didn't like it."

"Well, fuck him," Chops said. Sonny kicked some dirt up with his Docs.

"I guess he's mad cuz' some Ethiopian dude got beat up . . ."

The group all started laughing and high-fiving. "I did that shit!" Chops beat his chest. "Motherfucker is supposed be starving in Africa, took three hundred bucks off him."

"See," Smithy pointed at all of them. "You can't tell me there ain't no white boys in that area that don't need a job."

"Maybe he'll go home now," Chops led the laughter.

It made sense to Sonny. Every summer it looked like the Mexican army descended on the yards and gardens of Deerfield, and he wondered how many legal Americans were out of work. Sonny pointed at Chops. "They got no right to keep us away. They should give you a fuckin' award, protecting the neighborhood."

They all held up their beers. Sonny kept going, the anger he felt talking to Tracy ready to explode inside him again."Who the fuck does Marcus think he is? He doesn't want us there cuz' he is straight up scared of us."

Everyone yelled 'Yeah' at the same time. Sonny looked at their faces. Everyone was angry. *What is the point to anger if you don't act?*

Sonny drank the last of his beer and threw the can the fire. "What are we waiting for?"

"Huh?" Ace said confused.

"Let's go to Belmont." Sonny was adamant. Ace shook his head.

"Nah, man, we got a party goin' on."

"Race war right," Sonny shook his head. "If we're supposed be the front line in the race war we can't be afraid of a couple SHARPs "

"Tom'll be pissed . . ."

Sonny looked back at the house. Tom had been at the store since seven a.m. He was exhausted, and had disappeared into the house long before. Murphy leaned forward in his easy chair.

"Tom won't care if you kick some ass."

Sonny looked around. Ace suddenly looked a bit more sober. He couldn't be certain this was the best idea.

"Who has a car?"

SEVEN

"He's the King, King of the Skins.
Wot's his name? Joe Hawkins.
He's a Skinhead, he don't care.
Marten boots and short-cropped hair . . ."

—The Oppressed

Paul downed the last gulp of his second beer, just as an El train rattled the world around them. The only light they had in the back of the alley was an old punk t-shirt someone lit on fire and stuffed into an empty whiskey bottle.

He didn't hear Tracy laughing until the train was far enough north. Paul shook his head, feeling a little dizzy and tried hard not to show how fast the alcohol effected him.

Fifteen skinheads hung out under the train bridge that ran between the buildings. They were drinking and laughing. The longer Paul drank, the more he faded back into a a dark corner of the alley. Tracy leaned in closer as they talked.

Rooster walked into the Alley with a case of beer. Cheers went around. He looked at the new couple and laughed."Hey, Paulie? Can I call you Paulie?"

"For another beer, you can," Paul said, even though he was already worried about how he was going to not smell like beer when his Mom checked him at the door. Rooster threw him a beer.

"Hey, maybe you ought to slow down a bit," Tracy said quietly.

Paul gave her a 'Who, Me?' look. Rooster laughed and came up behind Tracy. "He's Skin. Let the boy have his fun."

Paul cracked open the beer, and took a tiny sip. Marcus leaned up against one steel pillar of the bridge.

48

"So, Paulie, did Trace tell you what she did back in the day, before she shaved her head?"

Paul realized that she hadn't. It was like life began when she shaved her head into a Chelsea cut. Tracy got up in Marcus' face, as close as she could considering he was so much taller. "Stop it, Marcus!"

"Ra-Ra, Go Team!" Cherry squeaked, setting off laughter. Paul didn't laugh. Tracy was hotter than any girl in his old high school, so why the hell not?

"That's awesome," Paul said. With boldness he didn't have two beers ago, he grabbed her waist and reeled her close to him. "I never dated a cheerleader before."

Suddenly, everyone gave them space. A southbound train took over the world. Tracy seized the earthquake-like passage of the train overhead and kissed Paul. It was sloppy and she tasted like beer. Once he relaxed, he felt her hand slide under his jacket,across his back. Her lips were soft, and Paul didn't want to scare her off. He kissed her gently, letting her lead.

Tracy pulled away as the train cruised away towards downtown. There was silence at first, then a few attempts to hold in laughter. Finally after a short round of laughter, the attention went back to drinking and off the new couple. Paul couldn't believe his luck.

"So, how does one go from cheerleader to Skinbird? And when do I get pictures?"

"Captain of the JV Cheer Squad, actually. My Mom was the Varsity cheer coach. She won a national championship, and I'm her only daughter."

"She was passing the torch, huh?" Paul asked through his drunken smile.

"Big-time," Tracy answered. "She wouldn't let me quit, so I got a punker boyfriend and matching mohawks."

"Oh, shit," Paul laughed. Tracy was warming to the tale."Yeah, she was embarrassed enough that I got my way. My cousin's super-Punk. He comes to Punkin' and hangs sometimes. So it wasn't totally weird to them. But Mom, she never got over it. What about yours?"

"They were hippies. So whenever they give me shit, I

remind them how my grandparents treated them."

"My Mom rubs my head and cries," Tracy told him with a devilish grin. They were laughing when they heard Smiley scream:"Marcus! MARCUS!"

The twelve-year old skin had stayed back at Punkin.' Marcus never let him drink with the boys. (The drinking age for Skins in that part of the world seemed to be a gray area around sixteen.) Looking every inch a miniature Skin, Smiley ran into the alley, still shouting. "Nazis! Fuckin' boneheads!"

Marcus stood up straight. Everyone stopped and looked. Smiley stopped right in front of Marcus. Shawna grabbed his shoulders.

"Calm down, leekle baldhead. How many of 'em ?"

To his credit, Smiley was calming down. "I don't know. A lot. A crew, at least ten."

Shawna looked at Marcus. "They're testing us."

Marcus crushed his empty beer can in his hand. Rooster pulled on a garbage bag that was stashed under a Dumpster, and pulled out three baseball bats

Smiley looked past Shawna at Marcus. "They're being super dicks, too."

Paul felt a nervous pit grow in his stomach. He'd never been a serious fight in his life. He was scared of the fight, but he couldn't leave.

If he left now he would look like a total wuss, not only to Tracy but the whole crew. He had to leave by ten if he was going to make it home in time. Paul looked at his watch, 9:42. SHIT.

***

It took them longer to find parking than the drive down there. Sonny almost lost his will to do this, and he knew Ace only came because he didn't want to look like a wimp to the other guys. His girlfriend Rachel wanted to come, but it ended up only being the guys.

Murphy, the oldest man in the crew, was the one that kept stoking the fire and keeping them pissed. He told them stories of the old days when they weren't afraid do what needed to be done. Calling them soft.

Sonny and Murphy took the lead, walking up Clark Street to the corner where it met Belmont. Only a small group of punks, and a skinhead that must have been a midget, were hanging out. The little guy ran off as soon he saw them.

The punks stared at them. The skaters just stopped. One of the skater kids looked Sonny up and down, and turned his skateboard around. He was ready to swing the skateboard like a club.

"Fucking pussies aren't even here," Ace said suddenly sounding confident.

"Just wait." Sonny knew they were off drinking in the alley.

Chops walked around breathing deeply. He wanted a fight. He didn't want to wait. He leaned over the skater. The skater was a quarter of his size. Sonny knew he would swing his board, but Chops didn't seem to be concerned.

"Hey, skate or die, dude," Chops was laughing, when the trucks holding the wheels on the bottom of the skateboard slammed into his skull. Chops fell over, dazed, but Smithy was behind him. Smithy punched the skater twice. The punches made two dull cracking noises.

The skater fell like a puppet with its strings cut. Two of the punks jumped in, but the Nazi threw punches too quickly. One of the punks took several hard punches to pull the skater out of the parking lot to the sidewalk.

Bleeding profusely from his head, Ace took off yelling to get the skater who hit him. The Manager ran out of the donut shop, screaming. Sonny turned around to tell the guy to shut up. The manager suddenly froze.

Sonny turned around just in time to see the bat strike, and the flash of white light.

***

Rooster ran down the street yelling, holding a bat high. The nightlife of Belmont cleared the sidewalks, even jumping into the streets. The drivers stuck in the bumper-to-bumper

51

traffic turned to watch the running gang of baldheads.

Paul couldn't help but cringe when Rooster swung and slammed his bat into the head of the first Nazi he could reach. The dude hit the pavement, and Rooster turned to the next one in line who nervously ran trying to tackle him.

Marcus ran to save the skater kid. A giant fat Nazi who was bleeding from his head savagely beat on him. Marcus swung low with the bat and hit the fat Nazi in the stomach so hard he keeled over and threw up what looked like beer and BBQ.

The skater tried to kick the fat guy as his friends pulled him away. Paul had never been in a big fight so he didn't know what to do. Then a Nazi came out of nowhere and punched Marcus.

It was a good punch that knocked him back on to the hood of an Oldsmobile parked on the street. The Nazi was diving for the bat Marcus dropped. Paul didn't have time to think, just stepped forward and kicked with his right Doc Marten. Paul felt the boot connect with the Nazi's face and heard bones crunch.

Paul grabbed the bat and held it high, as the Nazi skin spit blood and a few teeth.

***

Sonny lifted his face off the parking lot pavement, and felt some oil stick to his skin. He looked up in time to see Ace vomit. Murphy was takin' on the guy that batted him. He watched helplessly as Smithy reached for a bat on the sidewalk. A young-looking Skin kicked him in the face so hard Sonny felt his teeth hurt. Might have even been that midget. He didn't have time to see.

Sonny's head felt like it was going to fall off, but he forced himself up to help Smithy. The young kid raised the bat high and Sonny ran at him to tackle him. Just then, Tracy came up behind the young guy, her eyes burning with anger. It startled Sonny enough to stop him. Murphy grabbed Sonny's arm.

"Come on! We gotta get out of here!"

Sonny took a step back. Marcus stomped his right boot down on Ace, who was crying and screaming. Chops and Billy had to take a few blows to pull Ace back. It all became a blur as they tried to retreat back onto Clark Avenue. Flashing lights were coming from the west on Belmont. The SHARPs scrambled. The beatdown would have continued, if the cops weren't coming.

"My fucking jaw! Ahhh, fuck, my jaw!" Smithy screamed. Through all the chaos, with blood dripping down his forehead. Sonny saw Tracy. She reached up and grabbed the Skinhead that booted Smithy's head.

Tracy held his hand tight as they ran off. It was that moment that Sonny remembered that face, in the turnstile at the El when he saw Tracy.

***

"You have to get to the El!"

Tracy looked at her watch, just seconds after the police first flashed their sirens. Everyone scattered. Tracy grabbed Paul's hand and pulled him away. She took the bat,and flipped it to Marcus as he ran across the street to disappear in the far alley.

Then Tracy hid them behind a bunch of half-drunk Northwestern students who'd piled out of a bar to watch the fight. She pulled him down the street running. Paul looked at his watch: 9:58.

Tracy pulled him quickly down the sidewalk, weaving in and out of people. They still had to cross the street. "You got a token for the train?"

"Yeah —"

But she dragged him between honking cars. As they sprinted into the El station, he could hear the train rumbling south. Tracy handed him a few breath-mints and sprayed him with perfume, he coughed.

"For the beer smell," she apologetically waving the perfume out of his face.

The train was going over the drinking alley now. He only

53

had seconds to pass his fare and get up the steps. He reached in his pocket. He was almost in the turnstile when Tracy spun him around and kissed him.

Paul almost froze, having never been kissed so deeply. She pulled apart and pushed him in the turnstile. "Call me! Tomorrow!"

Paul spun through the turnstile as the doors to the train opened. He ran as fast as his Doc Martens would carry him up the stairs.

EIGHT

"How low can a punk get?"

—Bad Brains

Murphy took Smithy to the ER after he dropped the rest of the crew off at Tom's house. The party was over. Only the porch light and one light in the living room were on.

Sonny got out of the car and turned to walk back to his bunk at the store. The entire drive back to Blue Island was spent with Smithy screaming and crying, and Ace cursing under his breath.

The front door opened before the car was off. Tom stepped out on to the porch in a bathrobe. He was a quarter of the way through a cigar when he started walking down the steps toward the car. Sonny braced himself for a lecture.

"Not the kinda phone call I wanted to get tonight," Tom rasped. "You know, word's spreading pretty fast out there already."

Ace pointed at Sonny. "I told him it was a bad idea, Tom. I did. Ask anybody. I said, 'Tom don't want us down there yet.'" Ace looked around for someone to back him up. "Didn't I?"

Tom waved him off. "They just called from the hospital. Smithy lost six teeth. His jaw's going to be in a brace for purt-near six months."

Sonny felt guilt churn in his stomach like rotten butter. Tom walked up to him. "You realize you're going to have to cover at the store for him. You and Smithy are my only boys with a head for schoolin.'"

Sonny nodded. Ace was behind Tom, and seemed shocked. He'd been saying all week that he wanted to be a manager like Smithy. He'd worked at the store for three years. Sonny had only been there for a couple of days. Sonny knew Ace was lazy, and could barely count down the register.

Tom pointed at Sonny. "That being said, being smart for books don't mean you got a lick a' sense."

Sonny nodded again. He knew it was best to just listen to the lecture.

"Why was I telling you boys to wait? Huh?"

Rachel came walking down the porch. She didn't seem to run to her injured man. She stood behind Tom, and lit her cigarette. No one was sure how to answer, so a silence came over the yard.

"Ain't none of you got an answer?"

"We're building an army," Rachel said before taking a drag. Tom nodded.

"You don't build an army overnight, boys and girls. Adolf Hitler was a great man. He brought Germany back from the brink. Everybody wanted to stomp him down. We maybe the master race, but we ain't the majority on this planet. They was afraid of what Germany was becoming. What we can be. I ain't gonna question his heart, but maybe Germany moved into Poland too soon."

Ace nodded and pointed at Sonny. "I told you. I said it was too soon."

"Shut up," Rachel told Ace .She and Tom shared a look.

Ace didn't notice, but Sonny got the feeling Rachel and Tom were a little closer than met the eye. Tom smiled at Sonny.

"I ain't mad at you, son. You got balls the size of bowling balls. You're smart. Just need a little sense, is all."

Sonny nodded. Tom turned his back to them and started back toward the house. "Get some sleep."

Rachel followed Tom. She didn't seem bothered that Ace was beaten up. Sonny thought of his Dad, who'd almost lost his job because he could never collect the money he loaned out to the niggers and beaners. He hated his father for that. Dad risked the security of his family for what? Because was afraid to confront the scumbags who owed him money.

He couldn't believe what was happening."That's it?"

Tom stopped and turned around, eyebrow raised. Sonny kept talking. "They beat us down, put Smithy in the ER, and you say get some sleep? How about we figure out what it takes to kick their ass?"

"You're riled up, son. Put some ice on that head. Hit your bunk."

Ace ran after Tom, continuing to blame Sonny. Chops turned to Sonny and put out his hand.

"Don't sweat it, man. You're my brother now."

***

Paul's heart raced for the entire train ride south. He chewed all the Tic-Tacs Tracy gave him, and constantly checked his breath. He didn't smell beer. All he smelled was perfume.

A few times, people walked past him on the train and gave him funny looks. He just smiled and waved. When he finally walked up to his front door, he looked at his watch and cringed. 11:02

His parents were usually asleep by then, but presently he saw the dull glare of TV light in the living room. He held his breath and opened the door.

On the TV, Johnny Carson was interviewing Don Rickles, Dad was laughing. Mom looked at her watch. Paul held up two fingers.

"Two minutes, Ma! It was the El's fault, not mine."

Mom stood up and walked over to her son, about to hug him. She stopped, and waved fingers in front of her nose. His stomach pulled taut with tension.

"Oh, God, tell that girl to cut back on the perfume."

Paul laughed, and tried to run past her. His mother put her hand up. "Well, what's she like?"

"Amazing, Ma." Paul smiled. "Can't wait for you to meet her." As he spoke, he sidestepped her, made it to his room, shut the door and breathed a relaxed breath for the first time in a few hours.

Lying on the bed, he thought about how badly he needed a picture of Tracy. Paul reached down to start unlacing his

Docs when he got a first a look at the toe on his right Doc Marten.

It was scuffed up badly. He reached for his can of leather polish, turned on his desk light and got a good look at it.

Blood had dried on the lip of the boot sole, staining the yellow stitch red. There was a mark on the leather where a tooth had dragged across the boot.

Paul smiled as he shined them. In skinhead terms, there was no better way to break in a pair of Docs.

NINE

"For there's more money to be made
When it's made on the sweat of foreign slaves.
You can build your mansion on a hill,
With a view of the country that you killed . . ."

—Marching Orders

From the sky, it looked like the city never ended. It wasn't exactly where Klaus wanted to end up, but he hadn't made it to old age without taking risks.

He'd gotten used to speaking in Spanish. As much as he hated to admit it, in the past fifteen years he'd even begun to think in Spanish. He'd grown long-accustomed to the idea that he would die in Argentina, and merely hoped that the Odessa had a way to get his body back to the Fatherland for burial.

But now everything was all up in the air again. Klaus walked out of Customs, and relaxed. No one questioned his back-up Bolivian passport. Just as instructed, he dropped it in the trash as soon as he was out of the Customs officers' eye-shot.

Klaus smiled as soon as he saw the newcomer. He was older and wrinkled, but Klaus couldn't miss him. "Old friend," said Oswald Frick, with no hint of a German accent. Klaus smiled and pulled the man into a hug.

Frick was S.S. too, and had merely swapped uniforms with a green recruit to escape Germany. He'd been one of Hitler's early campus organizers. The son of a wealthy family in automobile production, Frick had founded early party flyers out of his personal fortune. Apparently the money was still coming.

59

"And you are?"

Frick cringed at the German accent Klaus had never fully shed. He looked around to make sure no one was watching, and handed an envelope to Klaus.

"A successful American businessman. I Told Odessa I would help you get set up in America, but then your on you're own."

"My own?" Klaus was surprised.

"There is another local business owner who offered to be your benefactor. It's best for all involved if you don't ask questions."

Klaus nodded. He'd never come that close to being caught before. As much as he wanted to argue, as much as he wanted to catch up with his old friend, he knew it was a bad idea. He could see that Frick had questions himself.

"Did you have a family?" Frick asked

Klaus shook his head. "What I did, I did for the families of Germany."

Klaus smiled. Some men went home at night from the camps to families, the love of their children. They didn't understand the men who had total commitment. "Some people never change, Oswald."

Frick cringed at hearing his birth name spoken in public.

"Everything you need is there," Frick said with a deep sigh, and turned to walk back through the terminal.

Overcome by emotions, Klaus wanted to stop him. The last time he saw Frick, they tortured a prisoner, discussed troop movements under their command, and ordered the deaths of two thousand men and women. My, how life had changed in the last forty-five years.

Klaus reached out grabbed his arm, leaned in and whispered, *"Heil Hitler."* Frick closed his eyes. For a moment, he looked like he was savoring a fine wine.

"You have nothing to be ashamed of." Klaus whispered

Very quietly, pulling his arm free, Frick whispered back. "I don't know what to think. But it is good to see you."

As soon as Frick disappeared into the crowd. Klaus opened the envelope. In it were a ring with four keys, including keys for an apartment and a car; a parking ticket with a parking-space number written on it, a sheet of paper with directions to his new home, and best of all, an Illinois driver's license. The picture was the same as his passport. The name was Kevin Cowl.

Klaus tried think about who Kevin Cowl was as he walked deeper into the airport terminal. A black woman smiled at him.

"Welcome to Chicago."

TEN

*"We'll show the world
that the boys are back to stay.
And you all know what we can do.
Heads held high, fighting
All the way . . ."*

—Cock Sparrer

Sonny was facing cans of WD40 when Tom came down the aisle. An old white lady was down the end of that aisle, comparing prices on Fix-a-Flat cans. They were the only people in the store.

In the three weeks that he'd been working the store, he stepped up for Smithy, playing Manager as if born to it. Ace was useless in the store. Even when he was on schedule, he often floated back to the storeroom to play video games.

Sonny ignored him. He didn't like Ace, but didn't want to confront him, so he just picked up the slack.

"Your shifted ended twenty minutes ago."

Sonny looked at his watch. 5:20. He shrugged his shoulders.

"You want overtime?"

Sonny shook his head. "Ace supposed to be on the clock?"

As if on cue, Ace must have passed another level on his video game. He yelled out, and you could hear a round of high-fives happening in the back. Tom shook his head.

"Sometimes I think that boy is part nigger."

Sonny cringed and looked up the aisle at the old woman. She looked more than a little disgusted. Tom didn't turn back toward her right away, but he saw the look on Sonny's face.

Racism out in the store was against the rules, no matter

62

how tempted you were to tell people off. Tom must not have seen her. "I'm sorry, ma'am," Tom said, putting his hands out. "Just a little joke."

The lady was not amused. She slapped down the can on the counter and walked out. As soon as the door shut, Tom laughed. Sonny laughed with him.

"Get Ace out on the floor," Tom told him, and walked over to help a customer who'd just come in and was headed for the far end of the store.

Sonny walked into the back room. Chops and Billy were lifting weights. Chops had 225 on bench press, puffing his way through it. Ace and Smithy were playing the game together. Rachel flipped through a magazine.

Smithy still looked funny, with the giant brace holding his jaw together. He couldn't talk and was pumped full of painkillers.

"Ace."

Ace kept playing. Smithy turned as much of his head as he could to look at Sonny. He was too doped- up to think straight. "I'm a little busy here, fresh-cut."

The insult brought a thick tension in the room, followed by silence. Chops racked the weight and wiped sweat off his forehead. Chops was about to defend Sonny. This was his problem, so Sonny put up his hands.

"Ace, I'm not sure if you've looked at the clock, but your shift started."

Smithy paused the game. Ace didn't look back at Sonny. He stared at Rachel. She barely looked up from her magazine. The expression she gave translated to '*Well?*'

"Boy, a couple days on the scene and suddenly you're King Skinhead."

Sonny stepped closer. "How about looking at me when you're talkin.'"

Ace stood up. He was in the worst shape of anyone in the crew, besides maybe his girlfriend. Sonny didn't see much challenge in him. His shirt read 'Champion Muff Diving Team.'

"I'm not King Skinhead, Ace. But Tom asked me to get

your lazy fat ass on the floor. I know you punched in, and you're not getting paid to play 'Donkey Kong.'"

Smithy pushed Ace's shoulder. He mumbled a sound through his wired jaw. Ace got close to Sonny's face as he walked past. He stopped for just a second. It was enough. Sonny kept his voice to a whisper, just between the two of them.

"I'm no fresh-cut. You watch that mouth, and put on a respectable T-shirt."

Ace punched the swinging doors as he went out on the floor. Rachel was the first to laugh. Pretty soon, everyone was laughing. Sonny wondered how Ace would feel, knowing his girlfriend was laughing at him. Chops beat his fist on his chest.

"Get this Skinhead a beer!"

***

Tracy sat in the open trunk of Rooster's car in the Punkin' Donuts parking lot when Paul came around the corner. He'd been counting down the hours until he could see her. Tracy ran up and jumped on him. He caught her, and she wrapped her legs around him.

They talked all week long on the phone, but in the three weeks they'd been an item they'd only seen each other for a few hours. He could only convince his parents to let him go to Belmont twice a week.

They met during the week for a date at Navy Pier, riding rides and eating junk-food. Tracy was supposed to be getting ready to leave for college, something she tried not to talk about.

They talked enough that Paul's mother got a second phone line so Paul could talk to her every night, long after both of them should have been asleep. He was young, but Paul made an impression. Booting a Nazi his first night on the scene helped. Dating the woman every single man in the scene wanted didn't hurt, either.

It also didn't hurt that Paul had a sense of humor. He was

the class clown who made everyone laugh. Shawna called him The Comedian. By week two, Paul felt like one of the boys.

But there was one problem. The North Side Boot Boys had a tradition called The Gauntlet. All of this because of this guy who used to hang on Belmont that everyone called Johnny Fuckhead.

They called him that because he had a little faded tattoo you could barely see done with a homemade Bic pen Tat gun that read: *Fuc*. It was right above his hairline, and faded. But when he started shaving his head and running with the Skins, you could clearly see it.

Around '86 or '87, Johnny Fuckhead claimed he was a Boot Boy. It didn't matter who they got in a fight with, or what happened, Johnny Fuckhead always went around back to make sure no one got away. One night he and Marcus were walking home from a 7-11, and they got jumped by three guys trying to mug them. Even then, Johnny Fuckhead ran off.

He wasn't welcome in the crew. Marcus decided if you wanted in the crew you had prove you were not afraid to stand up for your brothers and sisters.

After a kiss, Paul realized that Tracy looked worried. Marcus came up and tapped him on the shoulder.

"It's time."

Five minutes later, Paul looked at the skinheads lined up on each side of the alley. Guys seem to come out of the woodwork when they got a chance to beat someone into the crew. A few punched into their fists.

Paul couldn't believe he was doing this. He'd been in one fight in his life. His heart raced as he took slow steps. It wasn't a hot day, but he was sweating from inner fear. It burned hot inside him but he kept walking forward. *Just do it, get it over with.*

Tracy shook her head in disbelief at the end of the alley, She'd told him several times in the three weeks since they met that she thought The Gauntlet was a dumb tradition. She had to know he'd do it, new to town and living on the South

Side, it was crazy for Paul to even be invited to joined the North-side Boot Boys.

Paul stepped into the line. The members of the crew came at him long enough to give him a punch in the face. It became a blur of fists and flashing white lights.

Paul bounced back, trying to stand tall. It seemed like forever, but it was twenty seconds. Marcus and Tracy held each of his shoulders as Paul shook off the punches. He had a bruise forming over his right eye. Tracy used a Dunkin' Donuts napkin to wipe blood off his puffy bruised lip.

"Not so bad," Paul spit blood and laughed. "Is that all you North-Siders got?"

"Welcome to the Boot Boys," Marcus said and handed him a patch that was sewn with the image of two Docs kicking. He was going to have to ask his mom to sew it on his flight jacket. Everyone lifted their beer cans in the air.

"Oi! Oi! Oi!" They shouted and took drinks. Behind them suddenly a jam box came alive with Roy Ellis' signature hoarse bellow, "*I Want All You Skinheads . . .To Get Up On Your Feet . . .*"

But the voice was looped onto some up-tempo cover version of Symarip's "Skinhead Moonstomp", newer than Madness but not quite the most recent wave of revivalist Ska. Everyone started dancing in a circle, skanking to the beat. Tracy pulled at Paul. Tommy, one of the older skins, came up and punched Paul on the shoulder.

"Welcome to the crew. You took your licks like a man."

Noah came up behind both of them and slapped Paul's hand. "You had my vote the night you booted that Bonehead."

Marcus walked up, handing Paul a fancy-looking tweed cap. "From me and Shawna. For Ska shows, or whenever you're feeling rude."

Paul put on the hat and ran a finger across the bill. Tracy smiled big and Paul grabbed her hand. Rooster came over and whispered in Tracy's ear. Tracy hugged him and jumped around a bit. Rooster turned to Paul and smiled.

"From me and Cherry."

Tracy shook a pair of keys. Paul shook his head in

disbelief, still woozy from the punches. He and Tracy had never had a chance to be alone, and he had four hours before he had to be on the southbound El.

***

The key stuck in the door a little bit. The studio apartment was a few blocks up Clark, in a building across from Wrigley Field, above the Cubby Bear tavern. Music thudded dully below them as they walked into the apartment.

The kitchen was stacked with take-out boxes and beer cans, but the living space was clean enough. The futon was folded down into a bed, with clean sheets (a nice touch.)

A huge subway style poster of the Clash's "London Calling" took up one wall. Above the stereo and TV were a wall of flyers for shows by Agnostic Front, Cro-Mags, Naked Raygun, The Toasters, 7 Seconds and all kinds of other bands, dating back to 1984.

Paul looked at the flyers in disbelief. Tracy looked at a cassette holder filled with tapes.

Paul was nervous. He didn't want to admit Tracy that every attempt at romance back home had failed, although when they talked she'd figured that much out.

His first attempt at sex had been a disaster with the Red Hot Chili Peppers' album "Freaky Styley" as the soundtrack. He was dating a skater girl named Emily from St. Louis who came into town every summer to visit her aunt in Carbondale. She laughed at him when the blessed union was shorter than Flea's shortest bass solo.

Emily was the closest thing to a girlfriend Paul could manage in his hometown. Punk women or Skinbirds were beyond belief, about as realistic as dragons or hobbits. If you weren't driving a monster truck or star for one of the sports teams, the girls in his school were not interested.

Paul sat on the futon nervously buffing the toe on his boot. Tracy turned and looked at him, She was holding a tape in her hands. "You like the *Descendents?*"

He shrugged.

"Are you nervous?"

Paul shook his head, but he was nervous. Tracy thought it was cute. He just stood there and took twenty punches, but he was scared of her. She slapped the tape in and pushed Rewind, then sat down next to him. He put his hand on her cheek.

"Would you be freaked out if I said I love you?"

The tape player snapped, and tape rewound. She stood up. "At this point, I'd be freaked if you didn't." Tracy pushed Play. "This my favorite song by the Descendents. 'Hope.'"

A melodic punk song came on and Tracy danced in front of Paul like she was Polly Styrene, rolling a zine up and singing into the fake microphone, *"Someday, My day will come, I know one day I'll be the only one . . ."*

Paul tried to break in and kiss her. Tracy pushed him back onto the futon. As the last note of the song played, she lifted her Fred Perry shirt over her head and jumped on to Paul's lap. They kissed passionately as he tried to undo her bra.

He couldn't quite get it undone. Tracy laughed and balanced herself before reaching back and unsnapping the bra free. Paul swept it off her shoulder and she pushed him down, getting his own shirt off him before laying down to kiss him.

A fan blew gently in the window, but Paul felt like he was melting into her soft skin. Tracy kissed at his neck as she started to undo his belt buckle. Paul whispered into her ear, not wanting to sound stupid, "I . . . have to take off my boots."

His zipper came down. Tracy looked up at him.

"I don't see why."

ELEVEN

"Thirteen, fourteen, it's a teenage warning.
Fifteen, sixteen, but nobody's listening . . ."

—Angelic Upstarts

Paul made it past his parents, who didn't get off the couch when he came in the door. They didn't even notice he was fifteen minutes past curfew. He was pretty sure they were asleep.

Jack Hanna was on Carson with some kind of song-bird that landed on his head. The audience laughed. Thankfully, Mom and Dad were snoring.

Breakfast was another matter. They would get a good look at the bruises and the lip. Paul woke late and smelled waffles, his favorite. There was never a morning when he skipped waffles—he had to go down there.

He came into the kitchen, still wearing last night's jeans and wrinkled Cro-Mags shirt. His father ran the waffle iron and Mom read the *Tribune*. They weren't looking at him yet.

His father slid a plate of waffles at him. Paul sat it down in front of a waiting glass of OJ. He tried to eat as fast he could, before they looked at his face. Paul stuffed three bites worth into his mouth. His Mom folded the newspaper slightly, but still held it up.

"Would you men like to see that new Indiana Jones movie?"

"Uh-huh." Paul said as clearly as he could with a mouth over stuffed with waffles.

"I can't believe you haven't seen it yet, I mean, 'Raiders' was your favorite . . ."

Dad stopped when he saw Paul's face. Paul knew it

69

looked bloated and bruised, thanks to the waffles as much as punches.

"What happened?"

Mom put the paper down and gasped. Paul wanted to say 'It's not what you think,' but his mouth was too full. He put up his finger and chewed.

"Were you mugged? I knew that Belmont was dangerous . . ." Mom continued with various other ideas about what happened to her son. He couldn't say he was mugged in between here and Belmont. They would never let him go again. He couldn't say it was a fight, or the truth, because they wouldn't let him go either. He swallowed and gasped for air.

"It looks worse than it feels," Paul finally said, cutting his next bite. Mom scoffed.

"It looks awful. What happened, young man?" Paul hated when his Mom said 'young man.' It sounded awful.

"I was goofing around with some friends, boxing. I won't do it again."

Dad looked at Paul with a knowing grin. "Boxing? Really."

"Uh, yeah," Paul put a bite on his fork. "It was dumb. I won't do it again."

Mom and Dad looked at each other while Paul chewed. They didn't believe him. Mom gently tapped on the table.

"No Skinheads. Two weeks."

"What?" Paul dropped his fork. "Ma, those are my friends. And Tracy. You can't do that. Things are going awesome."

"Yeah, so awesome you're coming home with black eyes and split lips."

Paul looked cornered. "You can't do this." He felt angry, scared and sad, all at the same time.

"Oh, I don't think you leave us any choice."

Paul was almost shaking with anger. He got up, leaving his plate. His Mom gave him a look that should have stopped him in his tracks. A year ago, it would have.

Paul stormed out. As he hit the doorway, Margie Jackson called out, "Bring her here."

Paul stopped. He didn't say anything, just looked at her. She continued.

"You clear your plate like a responsible adult, do some work while you're grounded, and next Saturday she can come here. Watch movies, we'll have dinner."

Paul stood in the doorway and looked at his Dad. Dad pointed at Paul's abandoned plate.

"Best deal you're going to get, son."

TWELVE

"I don't like trendy cunts who pose.
Gonna punch you in the nose.
Stick my Marten in your crotch.
Don't like you. You're too much.
I'm evil, evil, evil, evil . . ."

—The 4-Skins

Ace had been at work on time all week. He was even was thoughtful enough to change out of his 'Harry's Bearded Clam Shack' shirt without being asked. After that day in the back room, Ace treated Sonny like they were old pals.

Ace had bigger things to worry about. Sometime during the week, Rachel broke up with him. Less than a day later, she and Tom made it clear they were some kind of a couple. It didn't seem to bother anyone in the crew that she betrayed Ace, who was less and less popular with each day, or that Tom was somewhere in his fifties and Rachel was just a few months over eighteen.

Rachel had been living in his house, in a room with Ace. Now the big guy was pretty much a roomie for Sonny at the store. Sonny didn't mind, as long as he did his job.

Ace came into the back room as Sonny was finishing his lunch. That meant Sonny was expected out on the floor. Ace sat down at the table, looking sad. Sonny didn't want to comfort him, or even touch his problems with a ten-foot pole.

"Can I ask you something, Sonny?"

Sonny stood, collecting his things. "I gotta get out there."

"Tom is a good talker, ain't he?"

Sonny sighed. He saw this coming. "Ace, I don't have time for this."

Ace ignored Sonny. "He talks all the time about race-war, but he don't never join us. Not for the fights."

"He's a businessman. Gotta keep up perceptions."

"Yeah, about that." Ace nervously kicked his Docs together. "You know that the nigger that identified Chops?"

Sonny didn't say anything but he knew all about the Somali cab driver who identified at least one of the skinheads involved. The Feds got involved soon after, coming by the store, harassing them.

"Man, that nigger fingered one of our guys. What did Tom do about?"

Sonny didn't say a word. Ace shook his head and continued. "I'll tell you what he did. Not a goddamn thing."

Sonny'd had enough. He turned, walking back into the store. Ace shouted after him,"Makes you wonder if he got the heart for the fight?!?"

***

Klaus turned the TV off in disgust. That Phil Donahue was a lying race-traitor sack of shit. He'd started to get used to life in Argentina. Now he was in the melting pot, watching the multi-cultural revolution and Zionist agenda unfold every day.

His apartment was nice enough. It looked lived-in, but the building was run down on the outside. He didn't know how to get a job, or what to do, so he sat in the apartment and practiced his rusty English by repeating what he heard on the TV.

His friends had all left behind their German lives, as if their time in the SS embarrassed and ashamed them. They tried to forget what happened, not just in their name but with their hands. Klaus didn't want to forget.

The first time he heard the Fuehrer speak, he was just a boy. His father had been killed in the Great War. When the Nazis came to power he was a teenager, as Hitler had been at the start of that war, angry and lost, without a father or mother to guide him.

73

His mother worked double shifts in a textile-mill for worthless deutschmarks. They had starved, and endured, waiting for a savior.

Adolf Hitler had passed him in an open motorcade, mere feet away, close enough to smell the polish on his jackboots, and feel the fire of those words upon him. Klaus fought to touch the touring-car, and then he was looking up at the great man.

The great man's eyes were tired. He was more pale than he was in pictures, and looked much older. He held up one imperious hand and bellowed: "HALT!" When the motor was silent and the crowd keeping their distance, the Leader of the Fatherland spoke directly to the adoring poor, who thronged him in that street.

The Fuehrer knew they were tired, hungry and desperate for Germany to be strong again. They'd suffered under the Treaty. He spoke to the suffering of the crowd, but Klaus always believed it was for him. That day, Hitler spoke to him.

It was only a matter of time before German strength returned as promised. That day, in the plaza in Munich, Klaus didn't really believe it could be done. Now he couldn't believe Germany had failed. He couldn't believe that so many of his friends try to deny the power of those times, the glory days of their lives when they came close to cleansing the world.

Klaus opened the small suitcase he'd kept since he fled the camp. The two pairs of clothes had changed, but the wolf-skin and his SS *Todtenkopf* cap remained.

Klaus put on the cap, looking at himself in the mirror. To himself, he looked old and beaten, but there was a time when he wielded such power. He was a monster, feared and loathed by his enemies, who considered him heartless,. That he could not deny. They had no idea who he was.

Now he hid alone in this apartment, dreaming of his glory days in the SS. A powerful anger grew inside him . . .

***

Ace stood behind the register with his braces up over his uniform shirt. Sonny had his head in a cabinet, counting inventory on spark plugs. Tom was over by the tires, wasting his time trying to sell top-of-the-line tires to some old buddy who just wanted retreads.

In between counts, Sonny had his eye on a black kid who came into the store a couple times a week and bought gum. That made Sonny suspicious. *Why not get gum at the 7-11?*

He watched in the mirror as the black kid slowly put a tool set into his low-riding pants. A few moments later, he walked toward the display of candy and gum set up by the register.

"Son of a bitch," Sonny whispered, walking quickly to beat the black kid to the register. Sonny gave Ace a look – Ace nodded silently understanding. *Stall him.* Sonny smiled at the black kid and walked across the floor to where Tom was just saying goodbye to his friend. Tom had a big smile on his face when Sonny walked up.

"That nigger up at the register," Sonny said in a whisper. "He has a tool set in his pants."

Tom looked over Sonny's shoulder. Ace struggled to get the register tape in. The black kid put the stick of gum on the counter and a dollar. He looked back and saw Tom and Sonny walking closer. The kid looked nervously out the window.

"Keep the change, awwwright."

The black kid turned, walking quickly towards the door. Tom and Sonny ran to block him.

"Where you going, boy?"

"I ain't your boy."

The black kid was almost out of the store when Tom grabbed him by the shirt. Ace yelled "Busted!" from behind the counter. The rest of the boys that were hangin' in the back ran out to watch.

The black kid looked up at the massive arm holding him. A tattoo of a Klansman lighting a fire to a cross slid out from under the sleeve, staring back at him. Sonny smiled at this.

His father ignored people taking advantage of him every day. He turned away, and ignored them time after time. Finally he would see some justice dealt. The boys had gathered to watch. Everyone expected an old school whoppin.'

"I'm sorry, sorry . . ." the black kid begged. *Here come the excuses,* thought Sonny, He wanted to hit the guy himself.

"You have something that belongs to us," Tom stated. The kid nodded, pulling out the tool set. "I promise you'll never see me again. Just let me go. We ain't gotta call no cops."

Everyone laughed. The tool set dropped to the floor.

"What's your name, boy?"

"Curtis." He shook when he said it.

"You run now, Curtis, and don't ever come back." Tom let go of him. Both Ace and Sonny cursed at the same time. They couldn't believe Tom would just let this kid off.

Sonny reached up and grabbed Curtis by the collar, wishing he had gloves on. Tom's eyes got wide. Sonny couldn't believe this. Sonny held him in place, while Ace and the boys ran to the front of the store.

"What the fuck, Tom?" asked Ace. Sonny never thought Ace had it in him, but he kept going. "You gonna let this jungle-bunny piece of shit rip us off and walk?"

Tom was adamant. "We caught him. We don't want more trouble."

Ace looked shocked, but Sonny knew a lot of his newfound courage was anger. Ace had spent a lot of time this week thinking about Rachel and Tom together.

Ace stepped up to Tom. Sonny tightened his grip on Curtis, who couldn't have been more than fifteen years old. Curtis begged Sonny over and over to let him go, but Sonny watched Ace.

"We got trouble already. You let this boy run, and every nigger from three neighborhoods over gonna know you can steal here. Open fucking Season."

"Watch your tongue, boy."

Sonny had to admit he agreed with the fat kid. Ace shook his head.

"No. We's out there fighting on the front fuckin' lines. I

ain't never seen you lift a finger. Grand Wizard, my fat ass."

Rachel walked from the back. "Ace, you shut your mouth."

"Fuck you too, you whore." Ace didn't even look at her.

"That's enough, Ace," Tom said softly but clearly. "Sonny let go of that nigger."

Sonny considered it, but shook his head. "No we can't just let him go. At least call the police."

Ace laughed. "Yeah, call the Zionist shock troopers. Fuck that. You're the Grand Wizard. You got balls enough to fuck my girlfriend but not . . ."

Tom reached over, grabbed Curtis and shook him. Curtis cried and begged. Tom almost threw him into Ace.

"I was stringin' up niggers before your Daddy put it to your Momma. You the troops now, son. I am the fucking general."

Tom looked around at his boys. For the first time since Sonny arrived, he saw doubt in the eyes of the crew. Tom only had burning hatred in his eyes. He only needed a spark.

Curtis had gone past fear. He tried to kick Tom in his knee, the bum knee he got in 'Nam. Sonny cringed when Tom screamed in pain. He didn't let go of Curtis. With his free right arm, he punched as hard as he could.

"Yeah!" the crew cheered in joy. Tom punched Curtis so hard he spit blood before blacking out.

"Good enough for you, Fatty! Huh?"

Tom punched the boy again. And again. Sonny wasn't sure how many times he punched the boy, but when he stopped Curtis dropped to the floor of the store with a horrible thud.

Tom grew silent, and fell on the floor of his store looking at his blood-covered hands. His right hand looked like it was broken.

Sonny looked up at Smithy and Chops. "Take down all the posters in the back. Now!"

Rachel ran to Tom's side. "Get an ambulance. His hand is hurt."

THIRTEEN

"Now you know why we gotta know . . ."

—The Cro-Mags

The doorbell rang. Paul took off out of his room, and down the stairs. Mom was wiping her hands with a dishrag and coming out of the kitchen. Paul cut her off at the bottom of the stairs, trying to shoo her back. She shook her head.

"I want to meet her."

Paul rolled his eyes and opened the door as his Dad appeared behind him. Tracy jumped back a little, seeing both parents staring at her.

She wore a dress, and black tights. Her blond bangs came out from under a cute knit hat. She'd curled the long part of her Chelsea. You couldn't even tell her head was buzzed. Paul could tell she was nervous about making a good impression.

"Hi, Tracy. Welcome." Mom offered her a soda. Tracy accepted it, thanked her and walked into the living room, looking around at everything.

"You take the train down from Deerfield?"

Tracy shook her head nervously. "No, I, uh, drove down."

"Oh. I didn't know you were old enough to drive. Paulie just turned sixteen, himself."

"I'm already eighteen," Tracy told her. "Just graduated actually."

"Really? College plans?"

"Uh, yeah, Southern actually. Paul told me you taught there."

"Yeah, since Paulie was a baby . . .."

Paul sat there, silently holding Tracy's hand through forty-five minutes of Yadda, Yadda and small talk. Tracy handled it like an expert. She talked about wanting to study graphic design, and using her artistic skills. She asked Mom what she taught, and pretended to be very interested in Sociology. *You should meet Professor Blah Blah, and tell them you know Margie Jackson . . .*

It didn't feel like it was ever going to end, when Dad suggested they get started on some lunch. Paul grabbed Tracy's hand and pulled her up the stairs.

When they got into Paul's room and shut the door, he let out a deep breath. "Oh God, I never thought she would shut up."

Tracy looked around the room. Pages ripped out of THRASHER were taped up on the wall. She knew some of the pictures of Agnostic Front, Sick of It All and the Cro-Mags, among others. She gestured at his skateboard, which looked worn-down about the trucks from years of grinding curbs.

"You ever skate anymore?"

Paul shook his head. "It would kill my Docs." Now he couldn't picture leaving the house without them on.

Tracy smiled. "Too bad. I used to think skater boys were pretty hot."

Paul sat down on his bed. "Well, not Skinhead hot, right?"

Tracy laughed and realized this was the first time she saw him without Docs on. She unlaced hers and sat down on his bed.

Paul knew almost everyone was surprised that Tracy took a liking to him. You couldn't get more fresh- cut than him. She was older, about to start college. It wasn't until now, hearing so much about her going to school, that he really wondered.

"I like your room. Very Skinhead. I can smell the Doc polish."

Paul gave her a gentle kiss. In the other room, Dad stomped around extra-loud, a less than subtle reminder that he was nearby. Tracy laughed.

"So, Trace, I was wondering . . . Why me?"

"What do you mean?" She seemed to mean it.

"You're hot." Paul shrugged his shoulders. "You're older, I'm fresh cut—"

"Who proved himself enough to be a Boot Boy," Tracy pointed out, cocking her head slightly.

"True." Paul moved closer.

"Don't underestimate those mocha-skin good looks."

Paul smiled. But she wasn't done.

"And honestly, you're sweet, and kinda innocent. My last skinhead boyfriend was an angry macho asshole. Everything you're not."

Paul could have been offended by the suggestion that he wasn't macho, but it was Tracy saying 'last Skinhead boyfriend' that got his attention. That was something she never said before.

"Who was that?"

Tracy sighed."It doesn't matter."

It did. "Somebody in the crew?"

"No, God no. He was back home in Deerfield."

"Well, if he's skin, why doesn't he hang out?"

"You know, I don't feel comfortable talking about him."

Paul stood up and looked out the window. His Mom and dad were busy at the grill in the backyard. "Why is that? Did he hurt you?"

She hesitated."No, not really."

"So what's the big deal?"

Tracy stood up and held his hands. "Remember that guy Rooster hit with the bat at Punkin?'"

"Yeah, he fucked his shit up."Then Paul remembered that guy getting up and looking at them. He didn't want to believe it.

"Wait a second. You're talking about a Bonehead?" Paul shook his head and stepped back. When looked at her white skin, he felt an uncomfortable knot twist up in his stomach. "You fucked a Nazi?!?"

Tracy shook her hands, trying to get him to calm down. "He wasn't a Nazi when we were together. He . . . well, he went over to the Dark Side. No better way to put it."

Paul was still a little freaked-out, but also became amused when he thought about that guy learning they were a couple. "He know you have a half-black boyfriend?"

Tracy shrugged "Our Moms are still friends, but he doesn't talk to his parents anymore."

Something about that didn't scan. "You been asking about him?"

There was no guilt in her eyes, just a little in her voice. "Yeah, just because I wanted to know if he was okay after the fight."

This was anathema. "Why?"

Tracy threw up her hands. "Bonehead or not, we have a history. And he still has a good heart, even if he doesn't use it much." She looked down. "I'm . . .I'm Skin too, Paulie. Sometimes honor makes you do things you don't really want to do, that even your own friends wouldn't get. But honor's just part of who we —"

"Honor." Paul cut her off. "He's a fucking Nazi. Honor means shit to them."

Paul turned his back to her. Tracy came up and put her arms around him, whispering in his ear.

"I love you. You're the sweetest boy I've ever met." Then Tracy kissed that ear.

"He saw us together, " she murmured.

"This is going to be a problem."

Tracy turned him around and smiled. "Not for me."

"Lunch!" Mom called from downstairs. Paul shook his head.

"Nazi with a good heart. Give me a break . . ."

FOURTEEN

"Blame it on the youth. We're ready for you.
If they make a mistake, they'll cover it up
with some ridiculous lie.
Morning newspapers gloating on violence.
How many more will suffer and die?"

—Xtract

Curtis Marks was nineteen years old. His only next of kin was a grandmother who lived on the outskirts of Blue Island, right by a major El and bus station. She was senile, and depended on Curtis to take care of her. That was too bad for her, since he was a junkie.

This all came as a relief to Sonny. The media barely noticed the death of a junkie shoplifter. It was only found on page four of the *Tribune*'s Metro section, and didn't even make the *Sun-Times*.

Tom's hero status in the movement grew overnight. Throughout that long night, Murphy and Sonny hung out at the Cook County Jail, failing to post bail. A few of the cops were sympathetic, and just as many weren't.

Not long after the sun came up, it became clear that Tom wasn't getting out. Murphy suggested that they needed to be thinking of the store.

They had to stay open. They'd need money for a good lawyer, if Tom was going to beat this on self-defense. They all stayed firm on the story, five witnesses would testify that Curtis Marks pulled a handgun on Tom Mansford. Self-defense, They put the pistol in the boy's dead hand, and called the police.

The fact that Tom was still in jail was a bad sign. The

police didn't buy the story. It didn't help that one of the cops was some Jewbag Polack who knew all about Tom and his political views.

Sonny turned the key to the back door, with only ten minutes left before he'd have to open to store and keep it going. He walked in and saw Ace already in uniform, carrying out two boxes of tools onto the floor. Smithy was counting out the register, even though he wasn't cleared to work. Chops swept the floor. Rachel was on the couch asleep, while everyone else was pitching in.

Murphy walked around high-fiving and thanking everyone for supporting Tom. Sonny appeared to be the only one who read the morning paper, or thought about Curtis Marks. *Would his grandmother have a funeral? Did she have the money or the mental state to do it?* No one else seemed bothered by the whole thing. Ace suddenly forgave Tom, and seemed to turn over a new leaf. Overnight, it seemed like he developed a work ethic.

Chops came up and gave Sonny a brotherly pat on the shoulder. "What's the word?"

Rachel sat up, suddenly hanging on Sonny's response. He gave her a shitty look, before calling everyone back to the back room.

"Tom's not coming home today."

Curses went around. Rachel looked ready to cry.

"It was that Jew cop!" Chops barked. Ace nodded ruefully. "Like Tom always said, the Zionists find a way."

Sonny whistled to shut everyone up. "Murphy's working on the lawyer. Our job right now is to support Tom, like he always did us. We keep the store open."

Chops nodded. "Recruit new skins."

"Yeah, get stronger," Ace affirmed.

Sonny pointed to the front door. "First things first."

***

On the fifteenth of each month, a letter with no return address arrived with a money order. Once a month, he would get this money. It wasn't much, but the apartment was paid for. He wanted to thank the person behind the money, car and apartment, but had no idea who did it.

The Jewel grocery store in his neighborhood was dirty and understaffed. He wanted to stock up, but got frustrated when no one came to the butcher counter to help him. He rang the bell twice.

This neighborhood they found was awful. He didn't think America had shitholes like this. He forced Jews into better living conditions in Warsaw. He decided to just worry about breakfast, and grabbed a half-pint carton of milk and chocolate mini-donuts

When he came to the neighborhood, he passed the store because of the name. The problem was that it was the only functioning grocery store near his new apartment. Klaus walked out, stepped back in his Dodge, and rolled down the windows.

It was still morning, but it wouldn't be long before his apartment would heat up. His AC barely worked and the room felt like a prison, but he didn't know where to go.

Klaus Schroeder looked in the mirror. He'd grown old, but he still felt the power the Third Reich gave him. It still flowed inside him, waiting to burst. Yet there wasn't a person alive who knew or understood the real power he had. This was a disgrace.

He sat in his car and read the newspaper, eating the Hostess donuts slowly as he read. Gang crime, city task forces on gang crime, murder after murder. On the fourth page he stopped at a headline. He read it out loud.

"Store owner with Neo-Nazi ties arrested for killing shoplifter." He scanned the article and saw the name of the store. "Mansford Auto-parts . . . Blue Island."

For a fleeting moment, Klaus got excited. Blue Island was just south of his apartment a few miles. It made sense. Perhaps this was his benefactor? If not he was a like-minded person. Klaus was tired of living in the shadows. Maybe it was time to re-join the struggle.

He got up, leaving his car and walked to the front of the

store. The old man stepped into a phone booth, and picked up the phone book connected by a chain. It took a minute of scanning the auto-parts store ads but he found it and tore out the page.

***

Sonny smiled at the black woman, who must not have read the fourth page of the paper three days ago. Maybe she didn't care. He was sure they lost some customers, but they gained a few too. Some people didn't want to come out and actually say they approved of what Tom did. The sales in the store stayed steady.

"Thank you for coming in."

She smiled back, and walked out. Ace laughed and shook his head. Sonny wasn't sure about what. He was pleased at least that Ace had turned his 'Ten Tons of Fun' shirt with the arrow pointing at his dick shirt inside out. He still couldn't quite tuck the shirt into his pants over his belly.

Chops came up behind him. "*Thanks for coming in,*" he parrotted in a mocking tone.

Sonny turned away.

"That was sweet, Sonny. You got a thing for jungle bunnies?"

Sonny ignored Chops, Ace laughed about something else. "I got a joke. Listen, why don't black women wear panties to picnics?"

Sonny turned at the sound of the door chime. An old man walked slowly into the store. Sonny remembered him. He'd come in a few days before, and just walked around. He never bought anything, just smiled at them.

He walked toward the counter. Sonny shushed Ace and whispered.

"Shut up. Customer!"

Chops laughed and leaned closer to Ace. "Keep the flies off the watermelon," Ace whispered, but they both laughed loudly. Chops almost fell to the floor, slapping his knee. Sonny cringed.

85

"Hey, take a break!"

Chops and Ace looked at Sonny like he had insulted their mothers, but they walked in the back.

"What's his problem? I said it quietly . . ."

"I don't know, man." Chops sounded confused as they left.

Sonny turned back to see the old man near the counter. Sonny shuffled papers that didn't need to be shuffled. He felt nervous, like he was being judged, and had a feeling like he should stand at attention. This was not a feeble old man. He was tall, strong-looking, his hair was gray, his skin wrinkled slightly but he was impressive.

"Can I help you?"

The man spoke in a thick German accent. "Don't be so hard on your boys. I don't mind a good joke."

Sonny didn't know what to say. In the aftermath of Curtis Marks, keeping the political stuff and racism out of the store was more important than ever.

None of this was looking promising, and it made his head hurt. The cops traced the gun back to

Murphy. Even though it wasn't used in the murder, the DA was not one to ignore tampering with evidence or interfering with an investigation, and presently fishing for each and every extra charge he could hang on them for doing so.

The prosecutor cited the vast White Power network and set the bail over a million dollars. Tom was a flight risk. He said he worked alone, but everyone had to backpedal around the statements they gave to the police. They thought it looked like he had a gun.

The old man stood silently, staring. It made Sonny nervous.

"I would very much like to speak with the owner, please."

Sonny wasn't sure where this was headed. Some folks wanted to come support Tom, but more than once he and the boys had to ask screaming anti-racists to leave the store. Chops lost a tire-set sale to man who watched one of those scenes yesterday.

Sonny folded his arms. "I can take a message."

86

The old man shook his head. "Still behind bars. *Tch-tch*. That is a shame. I would love to meet him."

The old man smiled and turned to walk back to the door. He moved gracefully, very fit for a man of his age. When he got to the door he stopped, and turned around.

"We could've used a man like you."

Sonny didn't get a chance to ask who he meant by *'We.'* The old man waved, pushing the door open. "I'll be back."

Sonny watched the old man walk across the parking lot.

"What's your fucking problem?" Sonny turned to see Chops standing in the doorway to the back room. His tone was a surprise. Chops had been nice and supportive of him since the moment he walked in.

"Excuse me, we shouldn't . . ."

"The store is empty now. It was a joke."

Sonny looked up at the camera, wondering if anyone was watching from the back room. "We have to be careful, Chops."

"Do we? I'm tired of losing."

"What do you mean?"

"Tom in jail, Smithy with his jaw wired up. We need to go on the offensive."

Sonny was about to disagree, to point out they needed to focus on the store, when Ace and Rachel walked out. Rachel was holding a blue piece of paper. "He's right. Look at this."

Sonny took the blue flyer and looked at it. *Rock against Racism. Anti-Racist action benefit show at the Metro.* There was a listing of Oi, Ska and Hardcore bands playing. At the bottom was a picture of Curtis Marks and a caption "Stop the racist attacks."

Sonny threw it on the floor. They expected something to happen. They were looking for him to show them the strength that Tom lacked. "Ok, when is this show?"

"Two weeks," Rachel answered.

"We lay low until then, but we're going to that show . . ."

FIFTEEN

"Take 'em all. Take 'em all.
Put 'em up against a wall and shoot 'em.
Short and tall, watch 'em fall.
Come on, boys, take 'em all . . ."

—Cock Sparrer

It was the first Saturday after Paul's grounding ended. He and Tracy spent the day driving around the city doing tourist stuff, since Paul still hadn't yet seen a lot of Chicago. First was the Sears Tower, where they almost got escorted out for standing on the railing putting their faces on the glass and looking down. That was freaky. They ate fresh cut fries at Navy Pier, and rode rides.

At the Water Tower Mall, they actually got kicked out. Apparently, Paul riding the shopping cart and slamming it into walls was not as amusing to Mall Security as it was to Tracy. It was fine. They were about to leave anyway, to head up north for the Rock against Racism show.

A Skinhead hardcore band from Indiana called Stand Alone had just opened the show when they walked in. The mosh pit got started right away. The skins stomped around and into each other, in the most violent dancing Paul had ever seen.

Paul hadn't been to many shows in Carbondale. Most of the shows were college punk bands and didn't start until it was too late for him. The mosh pit was a hundred times larger than anything he'd ever seen before. It looked mostly like a swirling hurricane of bald heads and mohawks.

The crowd went nuts when the bass player started the opening bass line for Agnostic Front's song "Last Warning."

Knowing that Paul was a big AF fan, Rooster ran across the pit and dragged him through the bodies to the front. With a guitar-pick slide, the band kicked into the song. Rooster had his arm around Paul as they screamed the lyrics.

"When I try to do right, you always push down . . . Always on my back . . . Why do you hang around . . . "

A body slammed into Paul, knocking him back into the pit. He got low and stomped around the floor, moving through the mosh like a shark through crowded water.

The bodies flew at him. Through the pain and energy of the pit, Paul felt his anger at his parents disappear (at least while he danced around the floor). Through one song after another, Paul lost himself in the energy, until he looked up and the band was thanking everyone, and telling them to buy some of their shirts.

Paul ran to the table, where Tracy had already bought one and threw it at Paul. "You bought lunch. The shirt's on me." Around them, the crowd was piling out for fresh air or cigarettes, down the long Metro steps to Clark Avenue.

Tracy and Paul got separated in the crowd. Paul called out "Marco!" and from further up the line Tracy answered, "Polo!" A few people in the crowd laughed. Paul worked his captive audience as any class clown would. The line moved slowly, so when Paul followed up with what almost amounted to a stand-up comedy routine about farting in the line, the stairwell filled with laughter.

Once out on the street the hardcore crowd divided in social groups. One bubble of kids were in Chicago straight-edge Letterman jackets formed down the street. They came to see Billingsgate, who were the next band playing. Further north up the sidewalk, the skins grouped up and passed a lighter around as cigarettes got lit.

Of them, there were the Baldies, an anti-racist skin crew from Milwaukee; and the NISH (Northern Indiana Skinheads) and a few suburban skins from up north.

Paul felt a little odd not smoking, but Tracy didn't like the smell on his breath, and he knew honestly that he really just held them more than he actually smoked them. But for the

89

first time they kind of smelled good to him.

Through the haze of smoke on the sidewalk, Paul watched cars slowly cruising by. There were always too many cars in Wrigley-ville, so traffic never went very fast.

Then, just beyond the haze of smoke Paul saw him. Despite the summer heat, Tracy's ex sat wearing a bomber jacket in the shotgun seat of some old beater car, arm out the window displaying a patch showing the Stars & Bars of Dixie. The car stereo blared Skrewdriver's "After The Fire," and the car full of Nazis bobbed their heads to Ian Donaldson's racist blithering.

Paul saw them first but slowly the crowd turned around. Marcus and Shawna stepped to the front, Marcus put out his arms, inviting them to come back. "Drive on by, ya white-power *pussies!*"

One of the straight-edge guys walked down the sidewalk towards Marcus. "That's the third time they drove by," he told him. "We're in if you need some bodies."

Marcus shook his hand. "Nah, we got it." The Straight-Edge kid was adamant. "For real, we wanna help."

Marcus slapped hands with the X'ed up straight-edger and turned back to the crew. "Who wants a special assignment?"

Tracy almost had a heart attack when Paul raised his hand. Tracy pulled him aside.

"Dude. They want you to be bait."

Marcus waved Paul over. "Come on, man. I'll explain. We'll be right behind you . . ."

***

Sonny told Murphy to turn the car into the McDonald's parking lot. Chops kept saying "We need to a park and go over there." That was when two Sharps and a straight-edge kid appeared outside. One of the bands must have finished, because suddenly it looked like there were least fifty skins, maybe forty straight-edge kids. When push came to shove the edge kids would fight against them.

"There are too many," Sonny pointed out.

"You wanna go home?" asked Chops. "They saw us. We can't just go home."

"Sonny has a point." Murphy put the car in park. "There are five of us."

Sonny looked around. Anger and hatred boiled palpably through the inside of the car. Ace was still mad about getting knocked around last time. Sonny had been sore for weeks, so he felt it too. He thought about Smithy, who still couldn't talk. He was still drinking all his food, he'd lost weight, and was constantly doped-up on pain meds. Sonny started to let the anger flow a little.

"Hey, look," Billy called out from the back seat. Sonny turned and saw a Sharp walking into the parking lot. He expected to see the crew fall in behind him, but he walked alone. As he crossed under the light coming off the restaurant they could make him out.

Sonny couldn't believe his eyes. Young and mocha-skinned, this lone skinhead was the same guy he saw holding Tracy's hand. He was the one that booted Smithy. They all knew it. No one had to be reminded.

"He's a halfbreed," Ace laughed. "Talk about a whigger."

"He's alone," Murphy hit the steering wheel. "Well, boys? You want some revenge?"

The lone Sharp walked around the parking lot to the alley that crossed back behind Clark Avenue. Sonny knew that alley dead-ended less than a block in.

"Let's get him. Now!"

Sonny was the first one out of the car. Ace and Murphy followed behind him. The Sharp looked back, but tried not to look obvious as he walked into the alley. Sonny could sense the young guy's fear even if he was trying not to show it. "What a dumbass," Ace observed quietly.

Sonny was the first around the corner. In the dark of the alley he almost missed him, but then the SHARP walked under the light coming from the back of a apartment building. The SHARP walked his lonely path down the alley.

"Hey, Sharpie?"

He kept walking.

91

"I'm talking to you."

The Sharp skin turned around. "You owe us some teeth, whigger!" Sonny yelled at him.

The five White Power skins kept walking closer. "No where to go, mud-man. You walked into a dead end."

***

Paul watched them stepping closer, ignoring the tension turning to solid knots in his back muscles. He was sweating, but despite the summer heat he felt a chilly breeze coming off Lake Michigan and swirling in the dead-end alley.

The Nazis walked past a light coming from an apartment window, and for the first time Paul got a good look at them. The fat one wore a FBI (Female Body Inspector) t-shirt. The oldest one was barely dressed like a skin. The guy talking Paul remembered the guy running his mouth. *That's Sonny, Tracy's ex. Has to be.*

"You must be Sonny,"

Sonny tried not to react, but Paul smiled. *All part of the game.*

"I don't think I know you . . .but it sounds like Tracy's been talking about how much she misses me." Sonny told him.

Paul shook his head. "Nah, you know what they say 'once you go black.'"

Paul tried to sound confident, but slight fear slipped into his joke. Sonny and his crew were almost on him. He clenched his fists,praying that the plan had worked out, and stood where he was supposed to be.

He was just getting worried when he saw the straight-edge crew creeping up through the shadows behind the Nazis. Sonny clenched his fists.

"I'm collecting teeth, for Smithy. Then I don't want you ever touching Tracy again." He raised his fist up. Paul braced himself for the hit, and got ready to swing. The door to the Metro swung up to Sonny's left. Tracy held the door open.

"I think that's my call, Sonny."

He looked up at her just as Paul's fist connected with his jaw.

"The name's Paul."

***

Sonny stumbled back, and saw Marcus, Rooster and Cherry run past Tracy. Sonny tried to stand up, but Cherry kicked him in the gut. The force of her Docs knocked him back. Sonny looked up in time to see a group of straight-edge kids with the hoods on their sweatshirts up, blocking the alley. Skinhead after skinhead seemed to pile out of the club surrounding them. Ace was lying on the ground, holding his bleeding head.

"Sonny, I didn't expect this out of you." Marcus stepped a bit closer.

"You're not King Skinhead, Marcus."

"And you are?" Marcus quipped. Sonny looked up at Tracy, Paul walked over and put his arm around her.

"You killed a kid, Sonny." Marcus said, voice rumbling like they could have felt it in Jamaica.

"You're killing our culture. Destroying it, you get to have your Black Power, White Power is only fair, Marcus."

Murphy stepped closer to Marcus. "Fuck this." He pulled a battered .22, aiming it at Marcus' head.

Paul's jaw dropped. He tried to stand in front of Tracy, but she pushed him out of the way. Marcus grew wide-eyed, expecting the shot to come. Then Rooster stepped out of nowhere, the tap to the beer keg he'd never returned from last night still sticking out of his pocket, but not for long. Someone yelled. Murphy turned just in time to catch the tap across the face.

The gun fired. Marcus screamed and went on his big ass, clutching his shoulder, but the blood was trickling. Not spouting.

"Run!" the older Nazi screamed. Then all hell broke loose.

Two gunshots were fired in the air as the crowd scattered.

93

Sonny and another Nazi had to work together to lift the fat guy and run back through the straight-edgers. Tracy pulled Paul into the club. H he saw flashlights and a group of cops running inside.

"Oh shit," Paul said as he grabbed Tracy's hand and tried to duck out the back. He could hear and see bubble-gum lights at the end of the alley. He felt a hand on his shirt hold him in place. He looked back and saw it was a cop.

SIXTEEN

*"I'm trapped behind a world of hate
and no one sees inside."*

—Killing Time

They lost Billy. There'd been cops, SHARP skins and straight edge kids everywhere. The cops didn't take sides. They pepper-sprayed everyone in the alley, and nightsticks started swinging. Sonny just closed his eyes and pushed Ace, who was finally running on his own past the pepper spray. They were all screaming, but when they got to the parking lot, Murphy had already pulled up in the car.

"Where's Billy?" Sonny screamed.

"Come on! No time!" yelled Murphy.

Sirens and flashing lights came down the street as fast as cars moved out of the way. Murphy moved them into the line of traffic. Sonny was thankful he didn't have any white-power stickers on his car. They were bleeding, bruised and crying from the pepper spray. If any cops saw them, they were busted.

"Lay down!" Murphy instructed them. Sonny could only see the flashing lights pull up, and hear the sounds of the chaos back on the street. "You guys keep quiet and keep your heads down, and we'll get out of here."

Sonny felt the searing pain in his jaw and the stinging bite of the pepper spray. Now he knew the name of that stupid half-breed piece of shit who was fucking Tracy now. He wanted to scream. He just thought about the feeling of being punched by him, and let his anger build. And build . . .

***

It took them an hour and half to fight traffic and get back to Blue Island. They went to the store because the back room was stocked with hazardous-material cleaners and serious First Aid kits. Murphy had avoided being sprayed, so he called over to the house and talked to Rachel. She and Dana were soon on their way.

Sonny splashed his face with water. It seemed to activate the pepper spray. "We gotta get to a doctor!" Ace kept saying over and over.

Finally Dana, Smithy and Rachel arrived. Smithy couldn't say anything, but Sonny nodded at the anger he saw in his friend's eyes. Smithy knew where the burn cream was, and passed it around. After Sonny put it on his face and arms, he handed it to Dana, who applied it to Chops as he cursed.

Sonny got so frustrated that he couldn't listen to them anymore. He stepped out in the dark front room of the store and sat on the stool by the register. His skin still burned, but it wasn't as bad as before. Just a dull pain, like a really bad sunburn.

The anger and the shame felt worse. They lost another round. He just wanted to sit in the dark and try to have a little peace. But there'd have to be revenge now.

They'd have to find Billy, who was still seventeen and probably arrested. He'd be sent back to his alcoholic father. Sonny wanted revenge as much as anyone, but he wasn't sure what they could do. They were outnumbered, and each time they seemed to come out of it worse.

Ace was in the back room, talking about bringing in skins from Detroit, or out in the country where things were more white-friendly. Sonny wasn't sure what to do. He just knew that this Paul kid represented everything he feared. Paul already had one white parent who married a black person. If he and Tracy got to together, it was another dilution of race. *His* Tracy. *His.*

Moodily, Sonny looked out into the orange light shining on their parking lot. A third car sat in the parking lot. "Hey,

96

Dana," he called quietly. Dana walked out into the dark store.
"You guys bring two cars here?"
Dana shook her head. Sonny pointed at the car.
"Whose car is that?"
Dana shrugged and walked into the back room. Chops
screamed for her help. Sonny stared at the car, trying to think
who it might belong to. *Did someone follow them back? Is
someone watching them?* He looked at his watch. It was
almost midnight. People didn't just park in their lot overnight.
Sonny was staring at the car when the door popped open.
He jumped, his heart racing, and reached for the bat that Tom
had kept under the counter since the day the store opened.
A tall man got out of the car, walking through the dark
shadows of the parking lot. Sonny wanted to run to the back
room and tell them what was happening. *What if it was
nothing? Would they laugh at him?* Just as he hit the back
room doors, he heard a knock on the glass windows.
Knock, knock.
He didn't want to turn around. What if it was a cop, who
had come down here to arrest them? After Tom was arrested,
plenty of those cops wanted the whole crew in jail.
Knock, Knock. A little harder this time.
Sonny gripped the bat tight and turned around. It was
the old German. The one who'd been coming in since the
Curtis Marks beating. He never bought anything, just walked
around the store and stared at them.
The old man waved at him now. Sonny lowered the bat,
walked to the door and turned the lock.
"Sir, I don't know what . . ."
"*Ein tschuldigung*," The old man pushed past Sonny.
"Gather your men, I'm here to help you."

***

Sonny led Klaus into the back room. Everyone stopped what
they were doing, and looked up at them.
"Who is this fossil?" Ace asked.
Klaus stepped forward. He put his hands behind his back,

walking like he did during camp review forty-five years ago. "Shut your mouth and listen."

Murphy squinted a bit and watched him carefully. Klaus cleared his throat.

"I am Klaus —"

" . . . Schroeder, Gruppenfuhrer of SS at Auschwitz," Murphy said with a smile. He stepped forward and offered his hand. "At least until you were transferred to Muller's *Sicherheitsdienst.*"

Klaus took his hand. Murphy shook it intensely. Long obsessed with the S.S., Murphy was not your normal child of the Sixties. Klaus smiled at him.

"Your knowledge of the Reich is most impressive, Mister?"

"Just Murphy. What an honor I just assumed that . . ."

"I was dead," Klaus shook his head. "I have been in hiding. The Mossad and . . . a few others, they have means that render my own . . . advantages . . . irrelevant. This means nothing to you now. It will. Advantages or not, I am an old man, and only one. They are many. A hunted beast still hunting for a new pack. I am trusting you men and women to be my allies."

Looks were exchanged. Klaus kept walking the line. "Tonight was an embarrassing defeat."

"You saw what happened?" Ace asked meekly.

Klaus nodded. "The Aryan people were not rolled out of the dirt in Africa. We were forged in the icy north, like the steel of a trusted blade. God chose us to be warriors on behalf of this one true master race. Our armies may have fallen, but not for long, now. Tonight, though, we lost another battle."

Ace took Rachel's hand. She let him. Sonny looked at Smithy, his jaw wired shut. The anger came back to the surface. Sonny stepped forward.

"We can still win the war." Klaus patted Sonny on the shoulder. "Indeed, we will. All these years in hiding, I have held on to one of the greatest weapons the Reich has ever known. Now I curate it, if only as last of the pack, to keep it from falling into the hands of the Jew-bastards, or worse. It is a lonely life. You wouldn't believe what I do for a living . . . But no matter. It is still a power which can, and should, be shared."

Eyes grew wide in wonder. Sonny looked at Murphy. He was smiling like a kid with the keys to the candy store.

"Enough playing Nazi. Pretend is over." Klaus smiled at Dana, then shook Chops by his shoulder. "Can you embrace being a monster? If it means our people will survive? Can you starve a room full of the Jewish rats? Can you cast mud people into a fire? Will you rip them to shreds in your claws? Can you do it?"

Sonny stepped forward. He didn't fully understand how or why but he believed in his heart this man was here to help them . . .

SEVENTEEN

"Better set an example.
Set a better example . . ."

—Alton Ellis & the Flames

They were transferred to the Cook County Sheriff's Department and held at the County Jail. Paul watched as they marched Cherry and Tracy away. He was with Rooster for the entire drive over and during the fingerprinting process. When the deputy came to march him down to the holding tank, he shook his head at Paul and waved him forward.

"Come on, Adolf,"

"You serious?" Paul stood up and walked with the deputy. "On what planet do I look like a Nazi?"

The deputy flipped through some papers on his clipboard. "You're a skinhead right?"

"I'm not a Nazi, dude. Look at me. My Dad hung out with Fred Hampton, spent the Seventies with a Fro. They don't give many of those to white kids. I'm Black, at least half."

The deputy was an older guy. He had to remember the shooting of Fred Hampton. The deputy stopped in front of the big metal door to the Juvie holding-tank.

"It was my understanding young man that you skinheads were all about the South rising again and Hitler bullshit."

"No man, the original skinheads were black, like me. Not all skinheads are racist." He turned so the deputy could see the SKINHEADS AGAINST RACIAL PREJUDICE patch with the letters spelled out over a half-laurel wreath and the helmet of a Trojan warrior. The Deputy shrugged his shoulders and turned the key on the holding tank.

"I thought you were just confused. But I don't really care.

Your buddy in there, I think he feels different."

He opened the door to the holding-tank. A skin with his braces up over a Confederate Flag shirt sat on the long, uncomfortable metal bench. He was young, but a little bigger than Paul. Their eyes met.

Nazi skins were like boogeymen. He'd only seen them during the two fights. As an anti-racist skin you talked about them the same way Bears fans talk about Green Bay Packer fans. He never had to be locked in a room with one.

"This isn't a good idea." Paul whispered.

"Hey, I got rules. Minors can't stay with the adults. I only have one holding cell for you."

The Nazi looked at Paul as if to say *'What's the matter?'*

"You put me in there with him," Paul said louder this time. "Someone is getting hurt."

The problem was the someone was more than likely going to be a Paul. The Deputy pushed him into the cell.

"Your father is on the way Jackson. Just keep the peace for an hour."

Paul stepped into the cell. He relaxed when he saw one of the Straight Edge guys, although he had his head back and his eyes closed. Two young guys that looked like gangster rappers sat beside the door. The only person that had a reason to be scared was the Nazi.

Paul looked around. The door shut and locked behind him. The holding cell was all concrete, with a silver metal toilet in the corner and a drain in the middle of the floor. Paul puffed up his chest.

"What do we call you, Adolf?"

"Fuck you."

The gangsters laughed. "He said his name is Bill, earlier."

"Judging from the shirt we'll call him Billy Bob," Paul said. Everyone except Billy laughed and one of the gangsters slapped Paul's hand. Paul sat down near Billy. "Looks like we have a long night ahead of us."

"Fuck you, Half-rican!" Billy got up and moved to the far bench next to the toilet. "Yeah, really tough guy, you were scared to come in here before you saw your homeboys."

Paul felt his face get a little red. He wanted to defend himself, and the first thing he could think of was what he had done in the past. "Maybe you weren't there when I booted one of your buddies in the fuckin jaw."

The gangsters yelled. "Damn! You did that?"

Paul nodded. One of the Gangsters moved closer to Billy. "So, he eatin' real food yet? You know that boy drinks dinner . . ."

Billy got up again, but there was nowhere to sit now. Paul felt a little bad for him, just a little bit. He also realized he never thought once about the way the guy he kicked that night must have felt. Paul stood up and offered a seat to Billy.

"Go ahead man, sit down."

Billy slowly took the seat, but kept his eye on them. He didn't relax. For five silent minutes, Billy and Paul stared at each other. No one said a thing. Paul remembered a conversation he had with his Dad while they shot around a basketball.

"So, basically, you're rival gangs . . ."

"Nah, it's deeper. Like they're super-bad. They hurt people."

"So you hurt them before they can hurt others is that how it works. You know, during the war people said they had to burn down villages to save them."

"Come on, Dad, you were a Black Panther."

"Right. A lot of my brothers never came back. Maybe if we talked to the other side. Learned a little bit about each other, who knows."

Then he swished a long ball. Paul wasn't looking forward to seeing his Dad tonight, but maybe he could learn a thing or two from the old man.

"Where you from?" Paul asked Billy, who didn't say a word, so Paul kept going. "So, yeah, I'm not even from the city."

Then, somewhat bemused, Paul heard himself telling the bonehead about Carbondale and being the only skin in town. Billy didn't say a word, but he also didn't stop him.

"OK, so you don't want to tell me where you're from."

Billy said nothing, Paul smiled big. "That's cool man, but answer me this? Why White Power?"

"For real, dog," the shorter and more thickset of the two gangbangers, wearing a stocking as a cap jail-style, chimed in. "Hitler lost. Before you was an itch in your daddy's pants. So what's up?"

Paul nodded. "We ain't tryin' to be dicks, dude. Honestly, I want to understand."

Billy looked confused, suddenly. Paul got the sense that he didn't want to answer. He seemed embarrassed by something. Paul decided to break the ice again.

"So when I first became a skinhead, I lived down South, and nobody sold braces. I needed suspenders so I went to a thrift store because my Dad told me to go there. The only suspenders I could find, thick as rulers, were Max Headroom suspenders."

Billy laughed.

"They must have looked stupid as hell."

"Oh, yeah. I went to shows like that. Big bad skinhead selling New Coke."

By then they were both laughing. The El turnstile of their circumstances began to click, and reflect in the middle.

"Whatever you're not saying, it can't be sillier than that, dude. I told you about the suspenders. How'd you end up wearing that shirt?"

Billy took a deep breath, and almost stopped himself twice. "Tom, he was our leader before they put him in jail. He took care of me when my Dad . . ."

Billy stopped. Staring at Paul, he seemed to shift gears. The honesty and trust melted away.

"Tom taught us a lot. My Daddy owns a farm out past DeKalb. Tom taught me about how the liberals and Zionists work together to using the city as a base to prop up the mud races. That you people would come out of the cities and destroy our way of life."

"You can have the country, dawg. Shit."

"Country's fucked. We don't want it." Both of the gangsters laughed.

But Paul barely heard them. Understanding grew in his eyes like light. Like the very-fucking-unquiet Spirit of 1969, rattling chains of Ska through the chambers of his multiracial heart.

He tipped his head back, trying to relax. When he heard what he said next, and really thought about it later, he reflected that it was the most truly Skinhead thing that ever came out of his mouth. And that even his ex-Panther old man might have been proud to hear it.

"I don't think you really believe that, dude."

***

Time slows to a snail's crawl in a holding cell, and there's no more boring place on Earth. Paul got a quick lesson in just how boring it was. He had no idea how long he was asleep, when the door opened and a female deputy called his name.

Billy found a way to curl up on the bench and fell asleep. A part of Paul felt the need to say goodbye, but Billy seemed to revert to tough-guy Nazi mode very quickly. The straight-edge guy had been picked up by his mother. Billy would stay there with the gangsters, who were being transferred to Juvie in the morning.

Paul walked out into the waiting room. Dad was talking to the same deputy that put him in the holding cell. His father had taken the time to get dressed, and he looked like he was ready to teach a class. Actually, he looked better dressed than that.

Paul knew it was his dad's philosophy to 'Never give the racist pigs' anything bonus to look down on you for.' He probably also took his time to make his son sweat. Paul looked at his Docs, not his father. *Boy, they need a polish.*

"You're damn lucky I talked your mother into staying home." They stepped outside. His father handed him the envelope with his stuff. Paul pulled out his wallet chain and watch. 2:30 AM.

"It's not like you and Mom never went to jail." Paul muttered.

"Don't even. We were fighting to end a war, protect our rights."

"Dad, they're Nazis. They think we're a poison to their culture."

"It's gang warfare. Don't try and bullshit me."

As soon as they sat in the car, there was a total silence. Paul started to explain, but Dad just put his hand up. Paul sat silently while the car came on. They didn't move.

"I don't really care to hear excuses, son. You got arrested."

"Dad . . ."

"No more Skinheads, ever."

Paul's eyes got wide. His jaw dropped. His father didn't notice, because he still couldn't look at him.

"That's bullshit, Dad."

"Bullshit is being at the Cook County jail at two in the morning picking up your son. You will not worry us like this again."

"Dad . . ."

"Don't say a word. You'll have to see Tracy elsewhere. No more Belmont."

Paul leaned back and found himself missing the holding cell.

EIGHTEEN

"The local pub, it stands silent,
And all of this town will be soon . . ."

—Cockney Rejects

Sonny stepped out of Murphy's car. The silent calm of the forest's edge in the middle of the night soothed him, despite the pain and aching bones from the fights.

Klaus dug in the trunk of his car. Smithy and the crew assembled at the trailhead. The moon was high above them in the sky, tinted orange from Chicago's pollution. Another week and it would be full.

Then Klaus was coming toward them, with a folded cloak laid across his arms. He directed them down the path, into the small wildlife preserve that was the only wooded area within miles of the store.

When they reached the center of the grounds, they found a fire-pit. Klaus instructed Murphy to light the fire, which had been stacked and prepared before they arrived.

The flame rose quickly, giving the small gully in the woods an unearthly orange glow. The crew gathered in a circle around the fire.

Dana held on to Chops. Smithy stood close to the flames. Sonny stared at Klaus, who stood behind the fire, shadows clinging to his face. He looked around at the young blood. Sonny could see the passion in the old man's eyes.

"Long before you were born, after the Great War, the German people were in a time of crisis." Klaus spoke in a booming, powerful voice. "The Kaiser had failed. The Jews and the West worked together to destroy us. Why? Because they feared the Master Race."

Sonny still wasn't sure why they needed to come out to the woods, but Murphy and Smithy were excited enough, so he agreed. Now he stood there, captivated by Klaus' voice.

"It was a great battle between Good and Evil. Don't let the Jews convince who was evil. It is their job to misdirect you. Treachery is in their blood. Science and Magic are both weapons in this battle. When used by warriors it is often hard to tell them apart. Evil, a Jew no less, harnessed the atom to make bombs. Good, the Thule Society and those of us who helped them, once harnessed Magic to make us hunters, and assassins. This cloak has not been tested since just after the War. I have kept it safe." His teeth bared. "Until now. Until the time. Now."

Klaus stepped closer to the light of the fire. He wore the gray hide cloak over his shoulders. Dana gasped. There was something strange about the shape of his pupils, and his eyes had gone an inhuman, reflective yellow. Their light sprang up in the light of the flames behind him.

Sonny thought the light of the fire and his eyes were playing tricks on him. Klaus stared at him so intensely it felt like the old man had a grip inside his skull.

"For the last four years of the war, the greatest assassins of the Reich ruled the night. Powered by the magic of the Moon. Deadly, unstoppable hunters, with a lust for the blood of enemies. Some would call them monsters. A dangerous weapon for any army. But it's that strength you must embrace."

Klaus walked up to Chops, pointing at the swastika patch on his denim jacket. "They already think you are a monster, believe me."

The old man turned to Smithy, waving him forward. Smithy looked at Murphy, who nodded and encouraged him to go to Klaus. Sonny wasn't so sure.

"Come, young man. It will heal you, make you stronger."

The whole thing was so strange. Sonny looked around. He didn't see fear on any other faces. He saw the same kind of wonder that he did on little kids faces' when they go to an amusement park. Pure wonder, and excitement.

107

Smithy stepped forward. Klaus swung the cloak over him. Smithy pulled it tightly over his shoulders. Klaus spoke again.

"I carried this with me since the Russians first punched through our lines. My Commander entrusted me with its safe keeping. I took a blood oath. With my blood. My old . . . wolf . . . blood."

Smithy fell to one knee, but the cloak was warm, pulsing, coming to life and tightening around him. Smithy grunted through his wired-shut jaw.

Sonny stepped around to watch, as Smithy looked up. Smithy's faded blue eyes went as yellow as oil-lamps springing into terrible flame. He could hear the popcorn-pops of every wire in Smithy's jaw when, one by one, they snapped.

Sonny went to help him, but Klaus held him back with incredible strength, still speaking.

"It is the skin of Ophois, the Wolf-God of shadowy Egypt. A miracle from long ago, a preserved trophy from the battle at the temple of Lykopolis. Much stronger than a golden fleece, *nicht wahr?*"

A horrible scream of pain and pleasure came from Smithy as he opened his jaw wide. It held together. Sonny tried again to move toward him. Klaus held him back once more . . .

"Wait. The skin-walk begins here. The pure blood begins to tell." Incredibly, he giggled. "Observe."

Smithy dropped to the ground, his hands covered in fur, fusing into massive paws. In the dull light of the fire Smithy's body convulsed horribly. "What are you doing to him?" Sonny whispered, in a voice that felt like trying to find the scream that ends a nightmare. Murphy stepped forward.

"Making him strong, Sonny. Watch!"

Smithy tipped his head back as his body shifted on all fours, thickening. At some point, he'd shed most of his clothes, but the white wifebeater popped away last as the wires had done first in his jaw.

When had his back gotten so hairy, and gray, or . . .
Oh my God his face . . .

108

Smithy's new face turned to the Moon, jaw gone prognathous, nose and cheekbones thickened to a snout, lips and gums and facial flesh skinned back from teeth as sharp as a baboon's. Klaus whipped the cloak away, and a wolf ran free.

Ace jumped back as the unnaturally-large beast loped past him, and began to circle the fire pit. No one spoke. Shock washed over them. Sonny looked at Klaus, but couldn't find the words. The old man chuckled, breaking some of the tension.

"When the moon is fully in blood, anyone who kindles the blessing of Ophois is free to take its form. Wearing the skin gives you great power. No human weakness, only lupine strength. You will never again know pain in the same way, and can only be killed by silver and one or two elements close to it on the Periodic Table. I will show you more about that later. And only through the heart. Or from the wound of another who has also kindled Ophois' blessing in their own skin."

Murphy stepped forward. "I'm in." Klaus handed the cloak over. Murphy swung it around, and put it on. Bravado crossed to convulsion as he fell to the ground, under the cloak, bones crunched and rearranged themselves. Murphy grunted and kicked dirt, before throwing off the cloak.

He lifted his wolf head and howled at the moon. Klaus laughed as he picked up the cloak again. Wolf-Murphy joined Wolf-Smithy circling the fire pit. Sonny couldn't see the humanity in them. When he felt them brush by him, his first reaction was the natural fear anyone fears when confronted by a powerful wild creature.

Sonny and Dana both spun to watch the wolves circle. Dana muttered under her breath, something that sounded like 'no' and 'can't be.' Chops just shook his head.

Dana took off running back toward the cars. Wolf-Murphy stopped in her path and growled at her. Dana stepped backwards toward Chops. He rubbed her shoulders.

"Don't be afraid, honey."

Klaus walked with the cloak toward Sonny. "You told me,

Sonny, that you had to watch while the mud people exploited your father. Walked on him."

Sonny nodded.

"Now one of the rats from the mud makes love to your woman. I have smelled her on him."

Sonny felt a spike of anger as Klaus handed him the cloak. There was a palpable energy like static electricity arcing from it. He rubbed it in his hands.

"Imagine being able to track across miles, be the ultimate hunter. Together we can turn the tide of this struggle. Your father will never have to grovel to the lower dregs again, because we will make a white America." Klaus pointed to the wolves running around the fire. "An entirely new Master Race, with the minds of true Aryan warriors and the strength of wild beasts. We cannot be stopped. Not this time."

The wolves continued to circle. Klaus held his hands out. The flesh in his palms bubbled up into twisted pentagrams, again. His yellow eyes glowed across the darkness.

"Join us, Sonny and I will show you the beauty and the power of the night." The old man's hands became claws, as his blade-like fingernails grew out to fine points. "It . . . still works . . ." he growled, amazed, voice thickening as his face did awful things, teeth elongating . . . He was still trying to talk.

"Power . . . The Wolf-Reich is reborn, after the fire. Look on these works, ye mighty, and despair . . ."

The old wolf lifted his long, angular head to the sky, and howled into the endless sea of stars.

Sonny put on the cloak. It felt like a heated blanket, crawling and tightening around him. The world was suddenly gone.

All he could hear was his breath, and his heart beating. Faster. Too fast. Panting like a dog on a summer day. His heart almost burst from his chest.

He took in a breath, and every smell in the park passed through him. He could smell each of his friends, sense their movement by smell alone. He could almost taste the food they last ate as it came out their pores.

He didn't have a chance to enjoy these new sensations. His hands tingled, the bones cracking and crunching as they shifted under his skin. It didn't hurt, just felt strange.

He let go, let the feeling over take him as the hair around his body grew so fast it made him shake. He shook off the wolf skin, and Dana gasped. He sensed her heart beat faster. Sweat formed all over her body. It smelled so strong it was intoxicating.

The moon pulled on him, reshaping him. He looked at the moon. Strength flowed from it and he felt an urge growing, like an orgasm that worked its way to the surface despite whatever he tried to do to stop it. He felt a howl form in the pit of his stomach. He had to thank the Moon.

"*Ahhhwoooo . . .*"

It was like a warm hug on a cold day. Freedom he never felt before. He shed his torn clothes and walked his first steps as a wolf. Smithy and Murphy ran past him. Klaus came up beside him, now a full wolf and nudged him, pushing him to run.

As Sonny took off, bouncing quickly on all four legs, he felt amazing. They ran the circle around the fire as Chops was the next to pick up of the skin of Ophois.

111

NINETEEN

"Darkened streets, late at night.
The boys are getting ready to go.
Fifteen strong. You'd better get away.
Gonna be a hell of a show."

—The Business

The first two nights, Klaus took them deep into the woods. He had to teach them to embrace the animal inside of them without losing control. Sonny was surprised how much of his mind and ability to reason was intact after they transformed.

It wasn't as easy for everyone. Klaus didn't want them engaging the enemy until they learned control. The most overpowering of new sensations was the power of smell. There was an amazing amount of information carried by the wind that only the wolf half of their brains could immediately process.

On the third night, they hung in the shadows of the Chicago streets and alleys, learning to cut through the matrix of data, learning first to track each other. Ace and Sonny ran for miles, getting to a clearing west of the city and for the first time in several hours. They stepped off the pavement, into the grass of an old field on the edge of a small wooded area.

Sonny relaxed a little as the pads on the bottom of his paws landed on the soft grass. It felt better than pavement. Ace had run deep into the woods in front of him at an amazing speed. Even at a great distance, he was learning that you needed to sense the other members of the pack. Sonny thought of it as smell, at first but that word didn't quite describe what he was feeling. The night was filled with feelings and sensations that he couldn't explain.

It was easy to forgot who you had been during the day.

Klaus had taught them many things one of which was to focus on something human at all times. *It is easy to forget and become trapped.*

In the distance, Smithy and Rachel were tracking them, testing their skills.

Ace took off faster into the woods, the trees sped past them in a blur. A smell was pulling them forward. Ace was being pulled toward like magnet to metal. As they came out of the woods Sonny made sense of the data.

The smell was both sweet and a little rank. Sweat pooled with semen and vaginal fluid as the skins of lovers ground together. Ace had perched himself on a hill above the house. Sonny bounced up behind Ace, They could see further than they could if human.

Two shadows behind a curtain moved against each other, in a room just lit barely lit by a candle with a short, almost-gone wick. Sonny didn't need the curtain open. He could sense every motion.

The man came inside his lover, his penis going soft, yet the woman still slid herself across him still. Their bodies were shaking, her breath and heartbeat much faster than the man's. In another room, deeper in the house, a newborn squirmed as urine soaked the little boy's diaper. He would cry soon and interrupt the process of bringing a new brother or sister to life.

Sonny was so focused on this young family, he didn't pay attention to Ace beside him. His wolf body was expanding in the center as he pulled in deep breaths. He was preparing for a run.

Sonny looked at him. Ace drooled over his sharp teeth. A new odor oozed out of his pores.

Ace was overcome with bloodlust and sexual hunger. It was all new to Sonny, but the wolf part of his brain translated. Ace had always been an over-sexualized teenager raging with unchecked hormones, now this? Sonny forgot for a split second that he wasn't human, trying to form the word 'No.' Ace jumped and took off in a run toward the house.

Sonny took off after him. The house came toward them quickly. Sonny was stronger and faster. He tackled Ace, biting his neck so they spun out, and rolled into the side of the house with a bang, just seconds after the baby boy cried from the far side of the house. Ace snarled and clawed at Sonny, who kicked him off with his back legs.

A wide-eyed naked man peeked through the curtains and saw the wolves fighting. Sonny smelled the woman wiping herself off and putting on a robe. She'd walked to the far side of the house. Ace stood on all fours, his eyes glowing an unnatural color.

He kicked up dirt, want to jump at the house. Sonny stood in his way, growling so low that only Ace could hear him. The message was clear: *Back off.* Ace intended to kill this whole family.

The pack gathered at the top of the hill. One by one, Sonny smelled their arrival. He kept his eyes on Ace. A howl cut through the night. The sound traveled from a distance, but Sonny felt it deep inside.

It was Klaus, calling them home. It was too far away for the human ear, but the whole pack responded. Sonny waited for Ace, who backed up.

The nervous man was draining buckets of sweat, watching the giant wolf with murder in his eyes back away. Once Ace turned and took off in the direction of Blue Island, Sonny followed him.

"What are you afraid of?" Klaus yelled at the wolf in front of him. "Why deny the boy his conquest? His flesh?"

The sun poked over the summer sky. Klaus looked out into the yard behind the former home of Tom Mansford. The pack had assembled behind the house, each in various stages of transforming back to human form. It was a painful process, one that brought remorse with it. All day, they would wait for the moon to give them the strength to change.

It wasn't so different from addiction. The strength, the power, and the freedom was like nothing in the human world.

Klaus was already dressed, and walked among them as bones crunched, skin crawled. Sonny was the first into human form "You need control, but you also need the flesh. It is your strength."

Sonny looked at his hand. The skin grew apart, the claws retracting. He would feel them under the surface all day.

"The longer the blood of Ophois flows through your veins, the greater the control you will have. Soon you will not even need the moon."

Klaus held Sonny's human hand. The young man shook. A part of him desired the change, but he couldn't call upon not in the light of dawn. Desire burned in his eyes, to throw off the shackles and run into the night.

"You will all be a cunning hunters, once you have the taste of raw blood," Klaus walked around the group. "But you must have control first. It is easy to lose who you are. Each time you let the wolf come to the surface, there is a danger that your soul will not let go. Many in my squad were never seen again, because their hearts would not return to the world."

Sonny looked at his naked skin. The scratches from Ace were deep, and they didn't heal like the other cuts. He still felt amazing strength, like he never had before.

He looked at Smithy. Muscles had appeared on the skinny young man that weren't there a day ago. Ace and Rachel's bodies had definition they didn't have before. The flab was gone. In its place, muscles tightened as they stretched.

Sonny flexed his new muscles and looked at Klaus. "I'm sorry."

"I gave you this strength, Sonny, to fight for our race, our survival. We need to be cold-blooded in this struggle. Do you think I lacked sympathy for the Jews under my command?"

No one said a word.

"I have sent thousands to the chambers to die. Worse than that, I worked them. I starved them. I had sympathy, but I knew in the end they were vermin. We can see what Hitler's loss meant to this world. The vile nature of this modern world."

Heads nodded in agreement. Smithy stepped forward. "Let us hunt tonight."

Klaus smiled. "I know whose blood you are thirsty for my friend. But first, we must be practical . . ."

TWENTY

"Look around at all the hate you see.
The color of your skin doesn't make a difference
To you or me . . ."

—Token Entry

The only time Paul got out of the house all week was to work in the garden or shoot hoops with his Dad in the back yard. He couldn't go see Tracy, and she was eighteen but still under her parent's roof and had lost the use of the family car. They talked on the phone every day, until Friday when Tracy took the train into town and returned to Belmont to hang with the crew.

That was the worst night. Paul sat at home with the VCR spinning tapes, ignoring the movies. He just stared at the clock, knowing that Tracy and the crew were gathered at Punkin. He talked his Mom into letting Tracy come over Saturday for the afternoon and dinner.

Tracy spent the weekend with Rooster and Cherry, and Paul counted down the minutes until one o'clock, when Tracy was due. The last fifteen minutes past one, he sat on the steps by their front door nervously tapping his foot. Dad walked by twice and laughed.

Finally, she knocked on the door. Paul swung it open and didn't even get a look at her, just hugged her tight. Mom came up behind them. "I've got lunch on the table."

Paul slid Tracy's backpack off her shoulder. "We're going put her pack in my room. We'll be right down."

They ran upstairs. As soon as they were in the room with the door shut, Tracy pushed Paul down on the bed. Their boots rubbed together as they kissed. They didn't have time for this, and their bodies ached.

116

"I don't want lunch," she whispered between kisses.

"We have to. Shit."

Tracy sat up and pushed her skirt down, trying to compose herself. Paul, sat up and smiled at her.

"God, you are gorgeous."

Tracy winked at him. "So, everyone says hi from Belmont."

Paul got a little red-faced. Being grounded wasn't exactly the mark of being a skinhead.

"Hey, it's okay. Everybody understands. Most of those guys wish their parents cared. They miss you, that's all."

Paul shrugged. "So what happened last night?"

"Well, some drunk guys, Northwestern students I think. One of them hit on Cherry at the 7 Seconds show at the Cubby. He straight up grabbed her tits. Cherry socked him good. Rooster got kicked out after he totaled the dude."

"No way, kicked out of the club downstairs from his place . . ."

"Yeah, so the frat brothers came looking for Rooster at Punkin' last night." Tracy smiled in the telling of the story.

Paul had a big smile on his face. Tracy could tell how badly he wished he could be there. Something bothered her all of a sudden. "It doesn't matter. I shouldn't tell you."

"It sounds hilarious. I wish I could have been there." Paul grinned.

Then Mom was calling them down for lunch. Tracy rubbed a scuff mark on her Docs and avoided Paul's eyes. "Kinda glad you weren't." Paul didn't conceal his surprise.

"What do you mean?"

Tracy motioned for Paul's hand. He gave it, but his heart almost stopped. Tracy was breaking up with him. He knew it. She was leaving for school, down to the town he escaped, where she was going to meet college boys. He hadn't expected it so soon . . .

Tracy took a deep breath. "Paul, I really do think I love you."

In turn, Paul finally exhaled.. Mom called out again. "I was glad you weren't there because I didn't have to worry

117

about you," Tracy continued with a nervous twitch.

"What?"

"You don't have to always be at the front of the line, you know," Tracy said with a little more conviction. Paul didn't know what to say.

"You don't have to prove anything," Tracy gripped his hand tighter. " Not to me, or the crew."

Paul stood up and beat his chest. "I'm a skinhead, okay? It's like that AF song. The blood, the honor and the truth. I gotta fight for my crew. "

"I know, sweetheart. I don't want to take that away. I just . . ." Tracy rubbed his shoulders. Paul looked away. "You know my parents are saying, 'No more skinheads. 'I threatened never to cut my hair again."

"Going for a Seventies look?" Tracy smiled.

"It's a protest. I'm speaking their language."

Tracy laughed. "Let's give them a week or so. I'll talk to your Mom, let her know I'm looking out for you."

"I'll still miss the Toasters show."

"I'll take pictures."

Dad knocked on the door, and opened it slightly. "Hey, burgers are up."

Paul grabbed Tracy's hand, and they followed his Dad.

"It's weird up there right now, anyways." Tracy whispered so Paul's Dad couldn't hear her. "A lot of the kids parents aren't letting them hang up north."

"What do you mean?"

"Because of the animal attack," Tracy explained.

"What?"

Tracy stopped him on the staircase. "Up by Wrigley. You didn't see that on the news?"

Now Paul remembered his Dad and Mom talking about something in their *blah-blah* language over dinner, but he hardly ever listened to them. "Some weirdo on WGN said it looked like a tiger attack." Tracy told him.

"A tiger? What?" Paul laughed in disbelief.

"Not funny, really. A Somali cab driver was killed."

Mom appeared at the bottom of the stairs. "Trace, that

skirt is so cute."

Tracy winked and went to give his Mom a hug. Paul forgot about lunch and ran down to the night stand where his parents left all the newspapers for the week. He hoped his Dad hadn't thrown them out already.

He picked up a stack of Tribunes and looked at the headlines, glancing back three days prior. Then he found it. Paul read the article.

The window was broken on the driver's side, and the cab driver, whose name was Abdu Seraw, was dragged out into the street. It happened at four in the morning, three blocks from anything residential. There were reports of screams.

A witness claimed to have seen a pack of wolves, but the experts of various government agencies and school around city agreed that was impossible. Paul thought the picture taken from the cab driver's license looked familiar.

"Hey, you coming in here?" Tracy asked.

Paul took the paper with him and showed it to Tracy. "Look familiar?"

"Yeah, it's the animal attack victim."

"Right." Paul nodded. "When we were at Cherry and Rooster's place."

"Yeah, that was nice," Tracy smiled. Paul kept going. "Remember I looked at that ARA newsletter, read about the fruit stand owner attacked by boneheads?"

Tracy grabbed the paper and stared at it. "No way." Paul knew she recognized him too. "That's the cab driver who told the police it was boneheads."

"That's weird."

Mom came walking into the living room with her fists on her hips. "Paul Jackson, your lunch is getting cold."

TWENTY-ONE

"A voice shouts loud: 'We'll never surrender.'
A voice in the crowd: 'Never surrender.'
A hand in the crowd's flying propaganda:
'Never surrender,
We'll never surrender.'
The Skins in the corner are staring at the bar.
The Rude Boys are dancing to some heavy heavy ska.
It's getting so hot people are dripping with sweat
The Punks in the corner are speeding like a jet,
Staring at the Rude Boys . . ."

—The Ruts

Sonny kept expecting to wake up. It was all so unbelievable. A week had passed since Klaus Schroeder came into their lives, but it went by like a blur.

At first, when they went into the night as a pack, it was like the world was a videotape stuck on fast-forward. The various new senses coming to life were still overwhelming. By the second night he understood why Klaus warned them about losing yourself.

It was like a high. Stuff like driving, watching TV, or even walking, felt so mundane. He wanted to be in the pack, to be a wolf, all the time.

They didn't all go out at once. They forced others to sleep, be ready for the store in the morning. It was a terrible feeling. Sitting at home watching TV, or listening to music, knowing the pack was out there. Still, no matter what what he did, it felt unreal. Like a dream. Sonny never woke up.

The pack waited, down in the backyard. He could hear the faint but familiar sounds of the Transformation happening.

He hadn't been with them on the night they found the cab driver. Tonight was his first real hunt.

Sonny reached in the bag he packed back at home and pulled out a vintage paperboy cap that Marcus traded him, back in the day. Sonny smelled the hat closely. He could smell his own smell, but there was the smell of Marcus still buried in the threads of the hat.

Sonny looked at himself in the mirror.

"Not King Skinhead for long . . ."

***

The horn section danced when they could. Marcus danced all night like a man half his age. His wife Shawna had never been a fan of Oi or hardcore, so Ska shows were a big deal. Marcus put on his best suit and porkpie hat and wore his braces up. Last but not least, he shined up his three-hole Docs for the night. The Vespa scooter got dusted and pulled out of the garage, and they showed up to the club in style.

Medusa's was a house club. They did shows from time to time. Tonight, it was packed with Ska fans from at least three states. The Toasters only had two shows in the Midwest all year, Chicago and Minneapolis, before the band headed out West. They were on their encore, and everyone was on pins and needles knowing they saved the song "East Side Beat."

The song started, and the skinheads locked arms to Chant "OI!" with the horn section. It was a daze, the last song. The dance floor swirled with old-timers and young people skanking to the beat. Marcus knew the song had about a minute left when he leaned over to Shawna. "Hey I'm gonna beat the crowd, pick up beer . . ."

Shawna didn't want to be bothered. She pushed him back and kept dancing. "See you at Rooster's!" Marcus shouted, but Shawna didn't hear him or even acknowledge him. Marcus used his size and height to push through the crowd and never lost his balance.

When he got to the long stairwell that lead down to the street, he laughed at how empty it was. He was used to

121

shuffling out like sardine at the end of shows.

On the street the night air felt chilly despite the summer humidity. He had, of course, walked out of an oven. He let his braces down and searched his pants pockets for his scooter keys.

His black Vespa was the third scooter in the line of fifteen parked in front of the club. It was shined up, with five mirrors set along the front, stickers for London scooter shops and the first Specials album cover on the wheel casing. Pain in the ass to maintain in the States, but Chicago had a shop where they worked on them, near Lincoln Park. Marcus had learned a thing or two about scooter repair, but the scooter didn't come out except special occasions, and a Toasters show qualified.

Marcus sat down on the Vespa. Just as he put the key in the ignition, he heard a growling dog. Marcus didn't turn the key.

He looked up, and saw an impossibly large dog on the sidewalk. It stepped close, into the light from the club. He thought it was a Husky at first, but this was no dog.

A wolf, but larger than one he had ever seen a picture of. Everyone in the neighborhood had been on edge since the cab driver was killed. It seemed likely this was animal that did it. Marcus wondered if it was rabid.

"Shit."

The band stopped. The crowd chanted, loud enough to be heard clearly down the stairs. They were stomping their boots, sounding like an army marching. *"One more song!"*

The wolf turned its head slightly, as if it was listening to the chant. It took small steps towards Marcus, staring straight at him.

Marcus didn't know shit about animals, so he didn't know what to do. It looked ready to pounce. Maybe the motor coming on would scare it away. Marcus turned the key, revving the small motor. The wolf arched its back, like it was ready to run.

Over the sound of the crowd chanting and motor of the scooter, he heard a faint chorus of growls from behind him. Marcus turned his head slightly, just enough to see three more wolves behind him on the street.

The crowd roared inside. The Toasters must have walked back on stage. Marcus shifted the scooter back off the kickstand. The wolf on the sidewalk pounced and swung its paws at the front of the scooter as Marcus peeled backwards.

There was an intense roar as his scooter slammed into the wolves behind him. He felt the hot breath of a beast fan his neck. A claw slashed at his side as he moved past them.

The scooter pulled back in the middle of Sheffield Street. Cab lights were bouncing down the street now. The light changed, a block away on Belmont.

Marcus felt a dull pain as he revved on the motor. The wolves jumped at him. The scooter squealed as it headed up the street. He pushed it as hard as he could. This was a side road, compared to Clark and Belmont, and empty at the moment. He thought he'd feel safer if he could make it to Clark Ave. and the busy bar scene.

He got the scooter going to thirty-five miles an hour, and the wolves ran with him. One flanked him on each side. The lights and sounds of Clark got closer. Marcus twisted the gas so tight he felt his muscles tighten. The wolves still ran beside him.

Marcus looked up, expecting to see Belmont Avenue. A wolf stood up straight on its back legs in the street. It looked seven feet tall. Marcus turned to avoid it, and crashed into a car parked on the street.

Marcus fell back, slamming his back on the pavement. Before he could scream in pain, he felt a paw at his shirt collar. The tall wolf had hold of him.

Marcus looked back to see the burning yellow eyes of the monster. It dragged him across the pavement toward an alley. The other wolves ran ahead of them.

He wanted to fight, but his back was shattered. Marcus felt nothing but pain pulsate through his body. And he couldn't feel his arms or legs.

The tall wolf stopped in the middle of the alley. Marcus tried to stand, but sharp new waves of pain were all he could feel. His racing thoughts turned to Shawna. *Would she be able to keep the house? Stay in the country? Could she keep the house?*

Marcus screamed as one of the wolves stepped over him, baring its teeth in his face. He felt more teeth tearing at his legs, at his stomach, like cats with a scratching-pad. He looked up at the sky between the buildings, and saw the nearly full moon before he closed his eyes forever.

***

Just before dawn, Sonny walked on naked human legs through the back door of Mansford Auto Parts. He proceeded into the storeroom bathroom, slammed the door and screamed.

Blood stained his mouth, and he felt gas churn the digesting pieces of human flesh in his belly. He'd fought for every scrap of Marcus he could get, eating his still-pumping heart raw. And he remembered it all now like the worst blackout drunk of his life.

He fell backwards to the toilet and hugged it, and felt pieces of Marcus climb their way back up his throat. He tasted acid bile and half-digested meat forcing their way through. Sonny's hands gripped the toilet seat, looking at the red-and-white mess floating in the bowl. He retched long after his stomach was empty of anything short of bile.

Sonny thought about staring Marcus down as he stepped on his scooter. The fear the man felt had filled him like warm soup on a winter's day. As good as that felt he couldn't stop shaking, looking at the dried blood on his hands. *Hands? What was he now?*

Chops came in the back door. "Whoohooo, shit!" Chops screamed with glee. He didn't sound upset, or bothered. Smithy came in next. He didn't say anything, but Sonny could trace his scent.

Sonny didn't move, just laid back against the toilet in shock. He could hear Smithy and Chops talking faintly. Smithy's jaw had healed during the first transformation. He had a lot to say after weeks of having his jaw wired. "Did you see how scared that nigger was?"

"Who's King Skinhead now!"

Murphy walked in, taking deep breaths.

"Oh my god, that is better than lynching, White mother-fuckin' Power."

Sonny held his hands over his ears. The dream was becoming a nightmare.

TWENTY-TWO

"The curtain has fallen.
Now you're on your own.
I won't return to you.
Forever, you will wait . . ."

—Andy & Joey

Paul had played basketball in his boots, but Dad was running over him. For the first time in a year, Paul slid into his Nikes and played one-on-one. Paul's hair hadn't grown out much, but he had shaved weekly since becoming a Skin, and Dad had made a few hippie jokes.

Mom wasn't backing off on the 'No Skinhead' punishment. Dad was trying anything to distract him. Dad offered to buy him a new skateboard, a guitar and lessons. She tried to introduce Paul to one of the neighborhood kids his age, and it made Paul worried about school. The kid was a total nerd.

The phone rang, and Paul stopped. His Dad blew past him and laid the ball in the basket easy. Paul ran towards the ringing phone. "Let your Mom get it," Dad called out.

"Could be Tracy."Paul ran up the back steps and opened the door. The phone on the kitchen predated them in the house by twenty-years, complete with its twisted cord and rotary dial. Mom,who was grading papers on the kitchen table, held the phone to her chest.

"She sounds upset," Mom whispered. Paul put his finger up, ran to his bedroom, extended the antenna and pushed the 'Phone' button. Tracy said hello in a pathetic voice, thick with snot and tears. Paul braced himself. "What's wrong?"

"It's Marcus, he's . . ."

126

Paul looked out the window. His father missed a long shot, and cursed. The ball bounced into the garden and Mom yelled at him. It took Tracy that long to finish.

". . .Gone. Just gone."

"What do you mean, *gone*?"

"He's dead. They found him this morning, what's left of him. He's all torn up."

"What?" Paul couldn't believe what he was hearing. He thought about the cab driver, and his connection to the Nazis.

Paul was scared and confused. He laid down on the bed, listening to Tracy weep, not sure what to say. He wanted to comfort her, but everything sounded hollow. The shock gave way quickly to anger in Paul. "Are you thinking what I'm thinking?"

Tracy sobbed, saying nothing.

"Who do the police think did this?"

"Animals. They don't know what kind."

"I do, it's the fuckin' boneheads."

There was a long silence. "What? They're morons, but not psycho freaks. He was torn to shreds, Paulie."

"They think Hitler's the shit. What's not psycho about that?"

"It's just, I don't think that . . ."

Tracy didn't finish her sentence but Paul had a feeling she was talking about her ex Sonny. He looked out the window at his parents. He didn't know what he was going to tell them, but he had to go.

"When's the funeral?"

***

"Ma, he was my friend."

"You barely knew the man, a few weeks at best."

Dad sat silently in the living room. He was using the *Tribune*, which Paul damn well knew he had read in the morning as a shield.

"Look, I can't get in trouble. Put on a tie, shine up my Docs, go to the funeral, and Tracy drives me home."

127

Mom nervously shuffled her papers. She didn't look at Paul, but kept her eyes to the dipping sun outside. "Skinheads are trouble, Paulie. Now one of them is dead. I can't let you be the next one."

Paul came through the kitchen and grabbed his mother's hand. She was not used to this kind of affection. Paul had been a Daddy's boy since he was very young. He could see her melting.

"This was a freak thing. Read the paper. Look, my friends need me at least this one time."

The paper folded in the living room. Paul kept his eyes locked with his mother, but he heard his father step up behind him. He could encourage her, but Mom had final judgment.

Mom had tears in her eyes. She was going to have to get tough. She cleared her throat."Tracy picks you up, and she drops you off as soon as the funeral is done. No Belmont."

Paul looked her in the eyes. "No Belmont."

He grew relieved. He couldn't be happy, not considering the circumstances. He turned and walked up the stairs to his bedroom, sat down at his desk chair and looked at the mirror besides the foot of his bed. The nappy hair had just started to grow out.

Paul reached into his desk drawer where he kept the industrial-sized hair clippers. He opened the plastic case, where the length guards lay unused. Paul didn't care what the newspaper or the TV news said about Marcus. He watched every news story he could. There wasn't a wild bear loose in the streets, or a misguided attempt to keep a pet tiger on the North Side.

He wasn't sure how, but the Nazis from Blue Island were involved. He was sure of that. Paul plugged in the clippers, and they snapped on with an intense buzz. He held the clippers on the edge of his hairline, staring into the mirror. He didn't care what his mother thought or if Tracy was afraid of him getting involved.

This was war.

Paul pulled the clippers across his head slowly and felt comfortable for the the first time in a week.

TWENTY-THREE

"The way you stand alone and proud,
The way you crop your hair,
Violence in your boots and braces,
Violence in your stare . . ."

—The Oppressed

Sonny sat nervously in a chair, next to a black mother and her two children. She had a little girl bouncing on her lap, and a five-year-old named Josh whom she tried to control with commands and snaps of her fingers. Sonny was one of the first people to show up for Cook County Jail visiting hours, and the mom was one of the last.

She sat down next to Sonny who reflexively looked for another open seat. With his heightened sense of smell, the waiting room smelled like a barn. Each drop of sweat carried with it a wealth of information. A distinct odor, that identified the person, but also carried hints of feelings and emotions. Anger, fear, sadness all dripped off people and danced in the air.

He looked at another woman, a Mexican who looked dressed up to be here. Sonny just wore a nice shirt and a pair of shined-up three-hole Docs he borrowed from Smithy. The whole scene disgusted him.

Welfare moms and criminal partners waited here to see the scumbags behind bars. Tom didn't deserve to be in this place. He tried to tell himself, as he had since it happened, that Tom was defending his store, that the kid was a drug-addicted burden to society. He assumed everyone of these losers were here for another burden on society.

The anger and hatred were comforting, an old friend.

Ever since they killed Marcus, he felt unsure of himself. No one wanted Marcus dead more than he did, but when they actually killed him, it was a different feeling all together.

The whole thing was so surreal and unbelievable, he felt like no one else took it seriously. Marcus was as hated by the Nazi skins as he was loved by the SHARPs The crew celebrated. Dana and Chops led the party like they'd won a championship. They drank themselves silly till the next night.

It was all fine, until the crew started to treat Klaus like a god. Considering what he'd done for them, the power it granted, that wasn't much of a stretch.

"You here to see your Daddy?"

Sonny turned toward the voice. The young black mother smiled at him, while bouncing her little girl. He remembered a joke Ace told him once about mistaking black babies for turd piles. The little girl smiled at Sonny, having no idea what he was thinking. Sonny shook his head.

"Just a friend."

"We goin' to see their Daddy."

The little boy rolled a Matchbox car along the floor into Sonny's foot. The little kid looked up at Sonny and froze. The mother snapped her fingers. "Joshua!"

The boy ran over, but didn't really look at his mother as she lectured him. Before he could blame it on their race, one of the white mothers went through an almost identical fight with a four-year-old boy across the waiting room.

Two hours had passed, and the room filled up with families waiting to visit. The young mother's name was Michelle. She worked two jobs, and was saving to go to college. When she sat down, he assumed she'd had that baby just to get more welfare.

"I gotta tell their Daddy it's over with us. He's bad news."

Sonny wasn't sure why she was still talking to him. He hadn't even responded to her besides a polite nod. He could smell her tension, fear. She wasn't afraid of him, but the guy on the other side of the wall.

Sonny looked up at her little son, He didn't look that

130

different from Curtis, the young boy Tom had killed.. Curtis didn't have a parent, but this little boy had a mother.

"Be strong for your little boy," he told her. At that, she smiled at Sonny and he sensed her relief. Then the big metal jail door opened, and a deputy came out. They called Sonny's number, and he let off a deep sigh.

She reached out and gripped Sonny's hand. He flinched. The woman laughed. "Thank you for being so sweet. Listening, I talked your ear off."

Sonny stood up, fixing his shirt. The staff read off a few other numbers. Sonny walked past several Mexicans and blacks, who stared at him through the glass of the cubicles. He couldn't smell them through the thick glass. At the end of the hallway, in the last cubicle, sat Tom Mansford.

His head was shaved like Mister Clean (*'straight up bic'ed'* as Tracy used to call it). He wore a loose- fitting orange jumpsuit, and smiled when he saw Sonny. They both picked up the phones.

"Sonny. Good to see a friendly face." Tom smiled. "They put me in a unit that's chock full of niggers on purpose, to drive me crazy."

"You alone in there?" Sonny looked around.

"There is a WAR skin from Detroit, waiting for trial. He works in the kitchen."

"That's good," Sonny nodded. "Better than nobody."

"WAR are good skins." Tom paused. "How's the store?"

"Good, sales are good. Good money for your lawyers. Smithy is back in charge. He got his brace off."

"Already?" Tom seemed surprised. Sonny nodded, not sure how to explain how he healed so fast. The reality was that he came here to try and tell Tom. He was scared about what was happening, and needed advice.

"I read in the paper that Marcus got fucked up," Tom laughed. "Too bad we couldn't do it first."

Sonny looked away from the phone, and winced. "It was us."

"What?" Tom was confused. "The paper said he was torn up by an animal."

131

Sonny couldn't say anything. He fought back tears and anger.

"What's going on, son?"

Sonny looked down the line. The deputy was at the end of the hall.

"Have you heard of an SS officer named Klaus Schroeder?"

Tom's eyes narrowed. Sonny spoke. "He was a commander . . ."

"At Auschwitz," Tom cut him off. "I know of him."

"Then you know he was never caught."

Tom looked down the aisle, then back at Sonny. "What does he have to do with Marcus?"

"He's here, in Chicago. He read about you killing the black boy."

"In self-defense." Tom pointed at Sonny.

Sonny nodded. "He came by to tell you he supported you and your actions."

Tom just listened. Sonny kept talking. "He's teaching the crew to be . . . I don't know, he has given us power. He said the Third Reich was interested in using dark magic."

Tom leaned closer to the glass, Sonny kept talking.

"He put us through a ritual, and it changed us."

Tom looked like he was about to squeeze the phone until it broke. He finally spoke. "Is he fucking Rachel?"

Sonny couldn't believe his ears. He stared through the glass, speechless. Tom pointed at him.

"Keep him away from my house, I'm getting out and Rachel is mine. She's a little big, but a girl that young is sweet as sugar."

Sonny almost slammed the phone down. He expected more from Tom than to just be a sicko chomo. Worst of all, he'd not heard a word he said.

"Tom, Klaus Schroeder wasn't lying about the dark magic. He's turned us into monsters, predators. We tore Marcus to shreds with our teeth."

Tom laughed. "Tell me does he have the Fuhrer's brain in a jar? Did he channel Himmler's ghost."

Sonny fought back tears. "Were in trouble Tom. Real trouble! This is serious shit . . ."

Tom laughed. "You're a good actor boy, but this ain't funny anymore. That ain't Klaus Schroeder. He's deader than dirt. That guy is some creepy pederass who likes young boys. Why would an old guy like that want to hang out with so many young men?"

Sonny sat back, staring through the glass at Tom. "Good question. One we didn't ask when you were still around."

"What's that supposed to mean?" Tom scowled.

"Some scary shit is happening to your crew. I need you to believe me."

"I don't know what game you're playing."

Sonny couldn't look at Tom. The fat man didn't believe him. It came through on the phone. Even through the double-reinforced bullet proof glass, Sonny's heightened sense of smell caught of whiff of the fat man's scent. It traveled around the air ducts.

He wasn't scared. He didn't believe a word of it. Worse, the distinct smell of sweat picked up slightly when the man mentioned Rachel. Even now he was horny for her. It was the thing he most cared about. She was young enough to be his child.

"He turned you into a monster, huh?" Tom chuckled. "Some kind of Frankenstein, or the Wolf-Man?"

Tom's mocking tone was like a finger, squeezing the trigger inside of Sonny. His heart raced, and he felt the moon pull on him. Just beyond the country jail walls, the moon climbed in the dusk sky. Sonny lifted his head, staring through yellow eyes.

Tom's jaw dropped. So did the phone. Sonny held up a hairy, clawed hand. He slammed his open palm into the glass.

Tom screamed as the glass shattered and spiderwebbed out in a pattern that hid Sonny from Tom's view. Tom slid his chair back, heart racing, as deputies on each side ran towards them. "What the hell, boy?" Tom yelled into the phone.

The deputies on Sonny's side grabbed his arms. He looked normal again. Somehow, he controlled the wolf fighting to

133

get out. Sonny pulled his arms free, and the deputies stepped back, surprised by his strength. All the other visitors along the hall were stunned into silence. Tom yelled into the phone.

"Wait, come back here son!"

Sonny pointed at Tom through the breaking glass.

"He did it."

The deputies didn't want to argue with Sonny. They sensed something inside him. The glass scattered, and Sonny watched as two guards pulled Tom Mansford away.

TWENTY-FOUR

"Pushed us too far. Gotta fight back.
Pushed us too far, choosing your fate . . ."

—Sick of it All

Shawna was a wreck. She seemed like a different person. Her tough exterior had melted away. She'd moved to the States only knowing Marcus, and now he was gone. Sure, she had the crew, and the crew were like family. But she never expected this to happen.

Shawna wept through the funeral, mostly on Cherry's shoulders, even once hugging the closed casket. Cherry held her hand throughout the ceremony. The crew was made up of hardened tough guys. Skins came from Milwaukee, Cincinnati, Indiana and St. Louis. Marcus was loved and respected. There were a lot of shaky lips, and attempts to hide tears.

After the funeral, the sun dipped low behind the city. They walked silent and somber down Belmont towards Lake Michigan. Noah had left the funeral early. When they got to the beach there was a small fire in a pit, and a cooler filled with beer.

Shawna walked past the fire and sat down, just beyond the waves coming onto the North Shore beach. Lights from ships out on the lake blinked in the coming night. Cherry sat beside her, but no one else had the courage to even speak to Shawna, who was a hair-trigger away from a meltdown.

Tracy squeezed Paul's hand as she passed him a beer. The skins from Cincy and St. Louis started their drive home, but they still had a larger group that usual. Smiley, the little kid skinhead, hadn't been around. Tracy looked at the little boy and back at Paul.

"Marcus was the father he didn't have. Smiley was eight when he lost his real Dad. This is gonna hurt just as bad."

The night was coming, and Tracy would have to get him home soon. He couldn't think of home. He only stared at the fire and thought about how much Marcus must have suffered. He felt the sadness and rage fight for his attention.

"Of all the crazy shit," Noah said, kicking sand.

"I know, so unbelievable," Rooster agreed.

Paul and Tracy shared a look. She shook her head, not wanting him to talk about it. Paul didn't know when he'd get this chance again. He was still technically grounded.

"I don't believe it. A tiger? Come on it's bullshit. This is Chicago, not Katmandu."

Tracy sighed and got up to walk towards the women by the water. "Paulie, we gotta go."

Paul shook his head and held up a finger. *Why did she call him Paulie?*

"You guys notice who the first victim was?" Paul continued.

Tracy stepped back towards the lake.

"I'm gonna hug Shawna, then we gotta go."

"The cab driver who identified the Boneheads." Paul ignored her again.

"Paulie, your Mom is gonna be pissed."

Paul cringed inside. He'd never been mad at Tracy before. Why didn't she just go for broke and say '*Your Mommy wants you home,*' Paul got red faced. Tracy instantly wanted it back. Noah nodded.

"I didn't think this was random. Never did."

Tracy walked to the water. She was angry. He knew she'd tried to keep him from talking about it. Paul waited till she was out of earshot.

"I don't know how, but those boneheads are involved."

Rooster and Noah shared a look. "You thinking we need to do something?" Rooster asked.

"Yeah, revenge," said Paul.

Rooster stood up, drinking his beer. "If you're right, this is murder. Not just murder. They fucked Marcus up."

Noah and Paul nodded. Rooster walked away. "I'm not sure I have it in me to respond just yet."

Noah tapped Paul on the knee. "Hey, man, Marcus was my brother, it ain't blood but it's just as deep."

Paul nodded.

"You know that they all work at an auto-parts store," Noah pointed west. "It's in Blue Island."

"I didn't know that."

"Well, that, Paulie, is where we find the fuckers."

Tracy walked back, wiping tears away. Shawna was weeping again on the beach. Cherry had her arms around her. Noah gave Paul a pat on the shoulder.

"You go home, bro."

"You'll give me call?"

Noah pounded his fist on his chest. Paul gave a half-hearted smile. He was going to have to figure a way to get out of the house.

TWENTY-FIVE

"A loser's way to find some friends.
You look like a skin, but that's where it ends . . ."

—Gorilla Biscuits

The store wasn't busy, Ace and Chops took a long lunch break. Since the Change, they were bored with video games. Smithy checked the inventory on tires, trying to feel busy, but the reality was all this mundane stuff was hard to do. Klaus told them they would get used to it, be able to control the urge to change, but now it was a challenge. No one wanted the life they had before.

The night as a wolf was vibrant and beautiful. The feeling of power and control that came with the hunt was unmatched by anything a normal human life had to offer. Time during the day slowed, and they all felt like they were walking through molasses.

"I'm gonna get Ace," Sonny said. Smithy looked at his watch, then shook his head.

Sonny walked to the back of the store. The TV and Nintendo, previously overworked, now sat neglected. The stereo over by the weightlifting rack blasted a vintage recording of "Deutschland Uber Alles." Sonny turned the corner to see Chops spotting Ace on the flat bench. The weight bar had every 45-pound weight they owned on it, as well all the tens and fives. He was pumping hundreds of pounds up and down with total ease.

Chops waved him closer, Ace counted as he pushed the weight. "Fifty-Two, Fifty- three . . ."

Rachel stepped closer. Now in the light Sonny almost didn't recognize her. The rolls of fat and extra chins were

138

gone. She wasn't thin, but toned. Muscles tightened under her skin as she posed. She looked at Sonny like he was a meal.

He could smell sex coming off of all four of the people in this room. It was a sent of uncontrolled animalistic passion. The smells of all four mingled in a way that made him queasy.

Sonny stood over Ace. Even he had slimmed down, his belly was gone. His 'Sorry about that thing with your daughter' shirt hung off him like a robe.

"Sixty-five, Sixty-Six . . ."

Ace ignored him, and continuing to pump the weight with ease.

"You going back to work today?"

Ace ignored him and kept pumping.

"Hey man, let him get a hundred," Chops laughed, pointing at him. "Sonny you gotta try it, it's crazy . . ."

Sonny felt his new muscles ache, and felt a eerie lack of control over his body. Dana came up behind Chops. He never thought she was cute before, but now she looked sultry. She blew him a kiss.

"Try it, Sonny."

Did she mean sex or the bench press? Sonny shook his head stepping back.

"Just get back to work." Sonny decided he would have to talk to Klaus about this. It was clear-they were not able to control their hormones. This was getting out of hand.

He stopped short of the back door when he smelled something beautiful. It sparked memories. Like the smell of a flower that had just bloomed, he breathed in deeply. It reminded him of Tracy, of better times. He felt a slight guilt, but it was overtaken by desire. He thought it was in his mind until he heard her voice.

"I don't want trouble. I just want to talk to Sonny."

Tracy was here, at the store. She was on the other side of the swinging doors, standing in front of Smithy. Sonny sensed something in Smithy, a raw kind of sexual excitement and hunger pouring out of his skin. The smell of his sexual yearning hung thick in the air.

He wasn't looking at Tracy, just wanting sex. He wanted

to lick the meat off her bones, as well. Sonny pushed through the swinging doors. Smithy jumped,looking at Sonny like his hand was in a forbidden cookie jar.

"What are you doing here, Trace?"

Tracy turned and looked at him. She took a silent involuntary step backwards.

What did she see inside me?

"Uh, Sonny," Tracy gulped. "Can we talk privately?"

Chops stepped out first from the back room. He looked at Tracy and licked his lips.

"Who do we have here?"

Sonny gave him a dirty stare, and Chops put up his hands. Rachel and Dana walked into the store. Dana sniffed the air. Rachel just stared at her.

"Everybody find some work to do." Sonny put his hand on Tracy's arm, she pulled it back. Laughter erupted as the group walked the store trying to look busy.

"You're okay. Come on, lets talk in the back."

They walked into the back room. Tracy cringed at the swastika flag over the TV. She looked around as the last notes on the Propaganda song came to their grand climax. Tracy gasped when see saw Ace. She remembered him from the fights, only weeks ago. He'd been enormous, and now he stood shirtless, cut like a Greek god.

"Ace, I need to speak to Tracy privately."

Ace toweled off and took his time walking past them. He stopped and stared down at Tracy.

"I remember you a bit . . ."

"Get out on the floor, now." Sonny pointed out the door. He didn't mean to, but he growled deeply. He had to concentrate to keep the beast inside him controlled. This was the first time he felt it during the day.

"It's cool," Ace smiled put on his shirt on and walked out into the store. Sonny pointed to the couch, but Tracy kept standing. "You should've called. Shouldn't have come here."

"You're right about that." Tracy looked around.

"Doesn't matter," Sonny smiled. "You're here, and I'm glad."

Tracy cringed, and made no attempt to hide it.

"What's happening, Sonny?"

Sonny looked at his Docs and couldn't bring himself to look at her. He never wanted to admit how angry he was at her. "I don't know where to start. How about we talk about why you're here? It's not because you miss me."

Tracy straightened up, tugging her shirt. "Killing Marcus was a stupid move. Every SHARP in the Midwest is ready to gun for you guys."

"We didn't kill Marcus. Don't you read the papers? It was a . . ." Sonny knew he didn't sound believable.

"Yeah, right, some kind of rabid animal that attacks rival skinheads and Somali cab drivers who just happen to have . . ."

"Listen to yourself." Sonny said in a condescending tone.

"How about you listen to me?" Tracy stepped closer. "You came down to Belmont. You were warned. You came anyways, and got your asses handed to you. You came back, I don't pretend to understand this latest psycho turn, but you seem to be dying to have this war."

Sonny was impressed with her courage. It was a bold move, coming down here. Somewhere in there, she was worried about him. She cared enough about him to warn him. Maybe she still loved him.

"Trace, I . . ." He tried to grab her hand. She yanked it away. It was like a slap. He didn't mean to, but he growled softly at her.

"What the fuck is wrong with you, Sonny? This bullshit," Tracy pointed at the Nazi flag. "This isn't you."

Sonny felt all his pent-up anger rush to the surface. He pointed at her, barely containing a fist. "I watched niggers rip off my Dad, year after year."

"Your Dad helped people, and just as many white people gave him problems. Forget your Dad. We both know what all this is about really."

Sonny scoffed. Tracy kept going. "This was all about me, and you know it."

Sonny shook his head. Tracy kept after him. "You did all

141

this to hurt me."

"Don't give yourself too much credit, sweetheart," Sonny said with a heartless tone.

"You're not like this," Tracy said, fear in her voice. Sonny looked at her, and in the back of his mind he saw her making love to her new boyfriend.

"Why don't you back to your half-breed?" Tracy just stared at him for a long moment. "He's a better person than you."

It both hurt and angered Sonny. He wanted to squeeze the life out of her. He had the power to do it. He felt the pull to change.

Energy traveled around his body like a fizzing soda about to spill over. Tracy shook, slightly. She was trying not to show it, but she was afraid. Sweat formed on her back, the muscles twisting into nervous knots. She was very scared of him.

"We don't need a warning, Trace. We'll win the war."

Sonny reached up and grabbed the back of her neck, pulling her toward his face with incredible strength. He stopped when she jammed a pepper-spray bottle in his face. She didn't fire it, just held it there.

Tracy stepped back. Sonny deflated like a balloon, dropped his face into his hands and cried. His hands had grown into claws.

"I'm sorry, Trace," Sonny looked up. Tracy turned around at the back exit door. Sonny hid his claws before she could see them.

"Your parents miss you, Sonny," Tracy said as she backed out the door.

Sonny stared at his hands. Fur covered them. The sharp nails were pointed like daggers. He failed to control it, even during the daylight. He wondered if Tracy had any idea how close he came to ending her life.

He smelled it now, becoming clear. The presence was there all along, but he was so focused on Tracy that he missed the distinct smell of a person who must have been hiding. Gentle footsteps carried the old man into the light. In the shadows of the dark storeroom he didn't seem like an old man, but looked tall and strong.

"I'm disappointed in you, Sonny." Schroeder's voice sounded angry.

"I didn't know . . ."

"I know you didn't. It was a mistake to let her leave."

Sonny didn't say anything. Klaus took a step into the light. "I don't blame you for loving her. It might surprise to know how many of my SS brothers took Jewish lovers during the war. I for one had a delicious affair with a woman named Tessa. Beautiful in a way her race did not deserve, I shot her husband, before he could get off the train. It's true, she never loved me, she wanted to save her children. She certainly had passion."

Sonny turned away, disgusted by the story. Klaus stepped closer and lifted Sonny's chin up. "She spied on me, learned my secret," Klaus smiled. "Our secret. In the end as much as a part of me loved her, I knew that she was an enemy of our people."

"What did you do?" Sonny asked in a meek voice.

"I dragged her screaming into the woods, and I ate her. There is a part of me that still misses her."

"Tracy warned us. I couldn't."

Klaus grabbed Sonny by the shirt and pulled him closer. "I will not lose again. This is just the first battle."

Sonny nodded. It was all he felt he could do.

"No excuses next time, Sonny."

TWENTY-SIX

"Skinhead, Skinhead, never give up.
Stick together, and act as one.
You never, never, never give up.
You stick together and act as one."

—Combat 84

Noah and the small crew he'd assembled waited outside Paul's house. From his parent's bedroom window, he saw Noah's Chevy parked down the street at seven PM, according to plan. Paul hadn't left his room all day, except to act woozy and sick at breakfast. His Mom came in twice to check on him, and he jumped into bed acting sick, as if he'd laid in bed watching "Star Wars" all day. He told her all he wanted to do was sleep.

They had the White Sox game on. Paul walked slowly through the house to the back door. All he had to do was make it out to the car. He didn't care if he got in trouble later, as long as he made it tonight on the mission. His Docs thumped on the ground too hard, so he walked in socks with his Docs under his arms. He would lace up in the car.

His father was asleep in his lounge chair. Mother was on the phone with Grandma. Perfect. Paul slipped out the back door, and even turned the deadbolt softly back to the locked position. It was an awkward run with his boots unlaced. As he galloped out to the car, the skinheads laughed. Paul shushed them as he got in.

Noah drove. Jimmy sat shotgun. Three northside suburban skins he didn't know were already stuffed in the backseat. They introduced themselves as Noah turned the corner and the stereo came on blasting "Hard Times" by the Cro-Mags. Bobby, John and Chuck. Paul remembered Chuck, Marcus

144

called him Chuckles.

They drove down the road, toward a freeway on-ramp "Glad you could make it, Paulie!" Noah screamed over the music.

"Wouldn't miss it for the world. Where's Rooster?"

"Don't worry about him. Oh, shit."The song chugged into the big sing-along. Noah turned it up as loud as his crappy stereo would go. They all yelled with the tape: *"Cro-mags! Skinhead! Breakout!"*

Noah turned down the stereo a bit, but still had to scream over it. "Yeah, man. That is what this is all about. Brotherhood!"

Forty-five minutes later, they pulled up and parked across the street from Mansford Auto Parts Store. 7:47 pm. Thirteen minutes till closing time. Everything was going as planned.

***

Sonny finished counting the register. As long as no one else came in, the hardest part of closing was done. Smithy stood next to him, nervously tapping his Docs on the floor. Klaus stood with his arms behind his back, nose in the air.

It was easy to imagine Klaus standing that way over looking a death camp. Sonny had no doubt he did it many times. "They're here," Klaus announced flatly.

Smithy ran to the front of the store in time to watch the headlights go out. Sonny looked at his watch. Thirteen minutes till closing. They were slow all day. He didn't expect any business before closing on a Friday night. He just hoped Tracy wasn't with them.

"One car. Fuckin' morons." Smithy laughed. "Looks like five of them."

Klaus stepped up to the counter next to the register. "Everyone in the back."

Smithy jumped at the command, Sonny looked at Klaus. The old man smiled.

"Just as we planned, young man, I will show you how delicious fear can be."

145

***

Noah turned around, looking at everyone in the car. "I'm leaving the keys under the mat, in case I get arrested or can't make it back to the car."

Paul nodded. They were filled with nervous energy. Everyone watched the seconds tick by until showtime.

"No civilians in there. Let's go!" said Chuckles.

Noah looked at Paul, who shrugged. They stepped out of the car. Noah opened the trunk with his extra key and passed out aluminum bats. They each carried a bat, walking calmly across the empty parking lot.

Noah signaled John, who picked up his pace and prepared to cover the back door. Paul felt his whole body shake as they walked up to the store. The neon Open sign flashed at them as Noah swung open the door.

They stepped in, one after the other, and stood in the doorway. The store appeared empty. Noah snapped his fingers at Bobby. All according to plan. Bobby wrapped a massive chain around the front doors, padlocked them shut. Noah turned the deadbolt to locked for extra measure.

Paul took the first swing, breaking the silence by knocking a set of paint cans on to the floor. Noah swung at the display of decals and bumper stickers in the opposite aisle.

"Hello. Were here to close your store!" Noah yelled. Paul and Bobby laughed. Chuckles took a few swings at displays.

Then the lights snapped out. Even the parking-lot lamps slowly dulled. The power had to have gone out. As the parking lot dulled, it became pitch-black inside the store.

Paul had never seen anything so dark. His heart raced, and then he remembered knocking over a flashlight display. Paul felt around on the floor for the flashlights. There was stock all over the floor.

"We know you killed Marcus. Why not come out and face us like men?" Noah called. Paul detected the fear Noah was trying to hide. The only sound was Paul searching for the flashlight. Then footsteps.

Paul found the flashlight, packaged with batteries. He

ripped open the package, and fumbled one of the batteries. "Shit," Paul muttered. Finally he scooped up the battery, shoving it in. The light came on, and they jumped back. A very tall old man stood directly in the beam of light, hands up.

Noah sighed and relaxed. "Where are the boneheads? The Nazi skins. We know they work here."

The old man stepped forward. "You've made a grave error," He kept his hands up. "These skinheads have joined my pack."

"Well lah-dee-fucking-dah," Paul said, as he stood up, pointing the light.

"You're right. We did kill your friend Marcus." Klaus grinned. Noah raised his bat in anger, taking a large stride forward. He only stopped when a chorus of deep growls like guard dogs came from every direction in the darkness.

Out in the night. In the distance there was a scream. The old man rolled his eyes. "Oh, I'm so sorry about your friend in the back. We killed him too."

The makeshift spotlight shook in Paul's hands as fear overtook him. Noah was frozen in place, staring at the old man. His eyes changed color in the spotlight, becoming yellow. Paul looked back at the door, cringing. They had padlocked it. Only Bobby had the key.

It was a trap. Klaus took a step forward. "This human race is weak, deluded, I will recruit from this army of skinheads and rebuild my pack. Just take comfort in knowing you will be the first sacrifice to the glory of the Wolf-Reich."

"Fuck you." Noah swung his bat at the old man. The bat never made contact. At the edge of the light, something like a dog pounced on him. Noah and the dog slid across the floor, and he screamed bloody murder.

Another of the creatures stepped into the light. It was a wolf. Paul dropped the flashlight and fell back screaming into a display. He picked the flashlight up in time to see the old man tearing through his clothes, suddenly covered in fur, face shifting as his howl rattled Paul's eardrums.

Chuckles ran forward and hit the half-wolf, half old-man

with his bat dead-center. The bat made a horrible sound on impact but the wolf-man just barked at him. The beast reared up seven feet tall and lifted Chuckles in the air. Chuckles kicked his feet uselessly until the wolf-man reached into his abdomen, pulling a claw full of organs free with a horrible ripping sound.

A scream came from behind Paul. He turned the light to see another wolf jump in the air and drag Bobby to the floor. Bobby screamed as a second wolf torn at him. Ribs became visible and innards dove to the floor, before Paul turned the light away from the whirling feasts. The sounds in the darkness grew intolerable. He ran to the front of the store and hit the doors.

Paul shook the chain links and heard the deadbolt clank. Then he heard a deep heavy breath, like a dog on a humid day. Paul turned the light around, and a wolf stared at him. It hesitated,locking into eye contact. It was all Paul could ask for.

He dropped the flashlight, and did his best Hank Arron. The bat went upside the wolf's head and it yelped. Paul turned, swinging even harder against the glass window beside the double doors. The glass shattered. Paul felt the humid air rush in. He jumped through the shattered glass into the night air.

Paul ran faster than he knew he could. Behind him, he heard the faint sounds of screams, and the running paws on pavement. The street lights on the next block were the closest light, just enough light to see Noah's Chevy.

Paul hit the car running, and pulled open the door fast getting out of the way. The door slammed into the wolf, knocking it back just enough. Paul slid into the driver's side and pushed the lock down. The wolf ran and jumped into the driver's side window, then hit it with massive force, shattering the window but not completely breaking it.

Paul reached across and pushed the other door's Lock button down. He reached under the mat, then pulled up the key, struggling to get it into the ignition, when the massive paw smashed the glass away. Paul turned the key.

When the car and lights came on he saw four wolves

bouncing toward him. The Cro-mags blared, overpowering the sound of the growling wolves. He slammed the car into Park, and hit the gas. He only had a Learners Permit and had never driven without his Dad.

It would have to do. The rubber burned on the pavement as he squealed out. "Fuck, fuck, fuck . . ."

Paul cursed as he took off down the road. In the rear-view mirror, he saw one wolf running after him just far enough back that he could barely see it. When he looked in the mirror again, he saw a large gash on his cheek.

He was speechless. Every bone in his body rattled with fear. He gripped the steering wheel so tightly he was afraid it would break in his hands. As he turned on to a major road, he swerved into traffic and a car honked loudly at him. The lights coming at him and the traffic should have scared him, made him nervous on his first real drive. It didn't. The nightmare he just escaped was still causing his heart to pound almost out of his chest. He had to get as far away as he could. Nothing else mattered.

TWENTY-SEVEN

"You've got the wrong enemy,
picking on a friend.
If we don't stand together,
then this is the end . . ."

—The Business

Paul sped toward the North Side. He couldn't go home. The only thing he could think of to do was to find Rooster.

The wind from the summer night blew around occasional pieces of the driver's side window. North of the city, lightning flashed as a storm came out of the west, one of those Midwestern summer storms that dump two inches of rain in an hour and shake the heavens with thunder.

Paul was nervous and freaked out, and drove slower than his grandmother. The last thing he needed was to get pulled over. He had no idea what he would say when he got there. Once he found parking in Wrigleyville, he sat in the car shaking and thinking about what he would say. His heart hadn't slowed a beat.

After a short walk to the building, Paul stared at the buzzer for a long moment. He pushed twice. An angry voice called back through the buzzer. "Hey?"

"Hey, Rooster. It's Paul."

"Hey, yeah, uh, this is isn't a good time . . ."

"I gotta talk. It's an emergency." The fear came through Paul's voice.

There was a pause. A disgruntled group of Cubs fans came out of the bar. One puked in the gutter, falling to the ground. Paul looked at his watch. It wasn't even eleven. He wondered if his Mom found him out yet. The door buzzed.

Paul ran up the stairs. Rooster waited shirtless in jeans at the door. "Better be important."

Paul came into the room. Cherry was barely dressed in a nightgown. She threw Rooster a Fred Perry shirt. Paul should have felt guilty for interrupting them, but he was too freaked to even notice. Paul paced the small living room. "I don't know what to say."

Rooster and Cherry shared a look. Cherry spoke first. "Noah told us about your uh . . . mission. We didn't think it was a good idea."

Paul tried to hold it in, but nerves tore him up. He fell in a chair and cried into his hands. "They're gone."

Cherry moved over and put her arm around Paul. "Hey, slow down."

Paul spoke as clear as he could through tears. "They ain't just fuckin' boneheads, they're something else. Animals,monsters, some crazy fucking things."

Paul watched through teary eyes as Rooster and Cherry shared a look. Paul shook his head. He knew they didn't believe a word he was saying.

"Come on. They tore up Marcus, and that fucking cab driver. They tore them to shreds."

Cherry put her hands up. "Stop!"

"No," Paul shook his finger. "I saw it, they got Noah, Bobby and Chuckles."

"What got them? What exactly are we talking about here?"

The door started to unlock. Paul jumped and fell back against the wall. Cherry put her hands up, trying to calm him down. "Woah, woah. Calm down. It's just Tracy."

"Trace?" Paul said, out of breath.

"She's the only other person with a key." said Rooster.

Paul felt both fear and relief. He wanted to see her, but she wouldn't be happy about what they did or that he hadn't told her. She was supposed to be over hanging out with the crew at Punkin' Donuts. Tracy struggled with the lock.

"What are we talking about, Paul?" Rooster asked again.

"I think . . . Werewolves."

151

Cherry's eyes grew wide, and she laughed as the door opened. Tracy walked in. Her expression was flat, enough to tell Paul she was furious. She didn't seem surprised to see Paul at all.

"Oh, my god, Nazi werewolves? That is the biggest pile of horse shit I've ever heard," Cherry scoffed.

"It's true," said an unfamilar voice from the hallway. Tracy held the door open as Sonny, her ex-boyfriend, walked in behind her.

Paul's instinct was to run, but there was nowhere to go. He simply froze. Cherry and Rooster stood up immediately getting in fighting stances. Paul struggled to grab anything he could use as a weapon. Tracy ran to him, but he moved away from her.

"You gotta lot of nerve showing your face around here," said Rooster. Cherry lunged at him, but Rooster stood in her way. Tracy tried hold Cherry. Cherry turned on Tracy.

"Fuck you, bringing a bonehead to my home."

But Tracy shook her head.

"It was my idea, I found her. Look, I'm trying to save his life." Sonny pointed at Paul. "You know what's out there. They're hunting you right now, and if Tracy didn't bring me, I wouldn't have beaten them here."

"We can handle your stupid little crew," said Cherry.

"We have, many times," Rooster added.

Sonny shook his head. "Things have changed. We have changed."

"That's an understatement," said Paul. Tracy came to his side, hugging him. Her anger for the time melted away when she saw claw marks ripped through the back of his shirt. Paul had been so amped he barely noticed the pain.

"He needs some of your blood. If they think he got you, they'll call off the hunt."

"This is such bullshit. This is Chicago not the Twilight Zone," said Rooster as he grabbed Sonny by his collar, and punched him in the face. The punch landed directly on his chin but Sonny's head barely moved. His eyes turned yellow, then glowed like stove coils. Rooster stepped back. Even

Cherry stepped back from Sonny.

Sonny put out his arms. The fur grew quickly, and his hands became claws as he held them out for them. Sonny let his deep growl break the silence first.

"Believe me now?" Sonny spoke in a deep inhuman voice.

Paul felt ashamed, shaking in his girlfriend's arms. He'd seen what those things could do. He understood, better than anyone. Tracy shook in his arms, too, and looked away from Sonny. Despite the fear he felt, Paul stood up and faced it. He knew, looking into the those eyes now, that he'd stared into them back at the auto-parts store.

"I didn't lie," Paul said through heavy breath. "Those things killed Noah."

"I let you escape," Sonny growled.

"Gee, thanks, but now you have to tell us how to fight them."

The fur retracted into his arm, with a subtle hiss. Sonny took strained breaths, as the friction burned on his skin. It looked like it took more effort to stay human. He nodded as soon as he returned to normal.

"I have a plan."

TWENTY-EIGHT

"I'm walking home tonight.
I only walk where there's lots of lights,
In the alleys and the doorways . . ."

–The Specials

Paul sat on a empty El train coach shaking its way across the south side of Chicago. He might have dozed off. He rubbed his eyes, looking out the window.

He didn't recognize anything. Outside was nothing but industrial landscape, factories and steel plants stretching for miles outside the window.

Slept through my stop! He jumped to his feet, realizing that the train car was empty.

It was a odd feeling, being alone on the train. The feeling of being chased was still warm in his memory. With each step it felt odd, like his boots were sticking to the floor. Everything felt off.

The lights on the train flickered on and off, like they would in a dance club. Paul ran to the door of the next car. The night air between the cars felt burning hot. The lights flickered faster. This time they snapped off. Towers at the factories spit massive plumes of flames into the night. This was the only light to crack the darkness.

In the dull orange glow, he saw the old man from the auto-parts store. When the next burst of flames lit the train car, the old man was gone, but a wolf ran at him. Paul ran to the next car.

He didn't hear the door open, but he felt the wolf behind him. He fell on the floor of the darkened train. He waited for the wolf to tear him to shreds, but only felt its breath on the

154

back of his neck.

Paul shook his head, suddenly aware he had to pee. He didn't jump up or scream like in the movies. He was just aware that he was face-planted into his pillow.

It took a second, but the feeling of a wolf's breath on him hadn't gone away. Now he jumped out of bed, looking at the clock. *3:35*

Only an hour since Tracy dropped him off. He quietly snuck back in the house. Only five minutes since he was calm enough to close his eyes. Sonny's warning played over and over in his mind.

They're hunting you now.

Paul sat up in his bed, stretching his cut and aching back. He couldn't sleep not tonight, not now.

Be patient. It'll work.

Being patient was the last thing Paul thought he could do.

* * *

Sonny walked into the store on all fours, with Paul's dried blood on his chin. He couldn't have fooled Klaus, so it was good he was still out running in the night with Dana and Chops.

Smithy was still a wolf when he sniffed Sonny's snout. They circled each other in celebration. It was more miles than Sonny cared to count, but he enjoyed every moment of the run. Mostly, he let the moon and the night guide him, bouncing from green area to expansive yard.

When he was wolf, nothing mattered but the hunt, the feeling of the run, the speed, and pleasure of the night air. Very few human concerns came to his mind. He wondered if he was doing the wrong thing. It was an amazing gift that Klaus had given him.

He thought of his human form, and called on it. Slowly the bones shifted and moved under his flesh. He felt the shape he'd taken for granted all his life now reforming. His wet, sweaty skin, suddenly bare of fur, felt freezing cold as he fell to the concrete floor in the back of the storeroom. He felt exhausted, weak and unhappy to be human again.

Sonny knew Smithy struggled with it. Rachel, Ace and Dana still enjoyed their time being human. They'd never in their whole lives felt good about themselves. As Sonny lay there, fighting sorrow over the return to his human body, he realized how petty they were. They were picked-on their whole lives, and talked about it all the time.

To them White Power was nothing more than a tool for excluding others. They were never accepted by their peers, so when Tom Mansford gave them a new family, a new purpose, they jumped in headfirst. When he was honest with himself, Sonny knew the hatred appealed to his anger. His anger at his father, his anger at Tracy.

The members of this crew were all damaged, hurt and mistreated, excluded or cast aside. The Nazi stuff gave them a channel for their anger, and a sense of belonging. It was okay before, when they were harmless. But Klaus Schroeder had given them real power.

Smithy sat up and stared at Sonny. He had the dried blood of the man who had broken his jaw on his lips. Smithy looked at him with palpable jealously.

"How did he taste?"

The question made Sonny uneasy, but he smiled. He had prepared to lie.

"Delicious."

TWENTY-NINE

"The warrior's brave, the warrior's cool
Even when he's got his back against the wall,
He's the king of the jungle"

—Last Resort

Sonny had been patient, working like nothing had changed for two days. Each night he ran with the wolves, it was harder and harder to come back. He wasn't happy with who he had become, what he represented.

Both days, he quietly worked in the store, and bit his tongue. Now that he'd really figured how and why these people came to this life, he had to fight back the urge to yell at them. To tell them how full of shit they were.

The phone rang. Sonny picked it up.

"Mansford Auto Parts. This is Sonny."

There was a pause on the other side.

"Hello?" He tried again.

"Hey, Sonny." The voice was so meek it took Sonny a moment to realize who it was.

"Hey, Billy!"

Smithy raised an eyebrow. "Wow, he's really missed all the fun."

"Billy, where you been? We haven't seen you since that night behind the Metro."

Billy paused again. Coughed, cleared his throat. "They called my Dad. He brought me back to the farm."

A part of Sonny was glad, but Billy's Dad was no saint. "He treat you all right?"

"Yeah. He was awful mad at first, but we had a good talk."

"That's great to hear, Billy."

157

Smithy rubbed his hands together. "Tell him he's gotta get back. Tonight is perfect."

Sonny knew Smithy's voice carried through the phone line. Billy heard Smithy loud and clear.

"Sonny, You think I should come back? I'm not sure I believe in this stuff anymore."

"Why is that, Billy? Be honest." Sonny said trying to keep his face flat, unreadable.

"The other Skinhead kid that was in jail with me, he was nice. I'm just not sure I believe the Jews and blacks are out to get us."

Sonny couldn't say what he needed to, with Smithy right there. He looked up at the time. Almost closing time. Sonny snapped at Smithy pointing at the clock, put his hand over the receiver.

"Hey, can you run to the back office and get me the night deposit bag?"

Smithy shrugged and walked off. Sonny followed his scent until he was behind two doors. He wouldn't have much time. With enhanced hearing, Smithy would hear every word.

"Billy, you listen to me and listen good. Don't come back. Some fucked-up shit has happened. If you talk to anyone else, they'll tell you it's awesome. Don't listen. Don't call again."

"What happened?"

He could smell Smithy heading towards the door.

"That's too bad about your Dad, Billy."

Sonny hung up the phone as Smithy handed him the deposit bag. The bell rang, and the front door opened. It was getting dark outside.

Klaus didn't need a cane. Not any more. But he walked with it to give the illusion of being a frail old man. He smiled. "The new members of the pack are waiting for us to start the ritual."

Smithy clapped his hands together. He rushed the closing duties. Klaus walked back out to the front of the store.

"New members? What's he talking about?" Smithy counted down the register, as soon as he finished the twenties he looked up.

158

"Yeah, Detroit Hammer Skins. Fourth Reich for real," Smithy let his eyes burn a inhuman shade of red. "For the true Master Race."

***

They walked through Tom Mansford's house. Klaus had truly moved in. It was cleaner than it had ever been under the previous occupant. Murphy and Tom collected Nazi artifacts, and now they were set up around the house like a museum of Schroeder's life. The Detroit Nazis, two carloads of them, walked around admiring the items when Sonny walked in.

They only stopped when the intense howling of wolves came from the back yard. The oldest of the Hammer Skins, a father figure named Dean, reacted strongly, but stayed silent on the surface. He had no idea they could detect his fear no matter how hard he tried to hide it.

Klaus reassured him. Sonny could smell the movement of the wolves in the back yard. Murphy, Dana, Chops, Ace, and Rachel had already begun to circle. They waited for the Ritual of Ophois to begin.

The moon pulled on him. Sonny sweated, trying to hold in the beast. Smithy didn't fight it. The fur was growing as he took off running for the backyard. If Sonny didn't stop this, they would grow too strong to resist. He had to follow his plan, and tonight.

Where is the Wolf-Skin? Sonny reached out with his senses, smelling for it. It was preserved thousands of years ago, had survived hundreds of battles fought over it. The sweat and blood of thousands, in the order and those were victims collected on the surface. The skin of Ophois had a distinct smell, no smell like it on earth.

There it was, sitting neatly folded on the dining-room table. Klaus lead Dean into the living room. Sonny followed behind them. "Murphy tells me you have studied the SS as intensely as he did," Klaus was saying.

Dean nodded. Something about Dean's scent told Sonny that Dean was skeptical of the old man, not sure if he trusted

159

or believed in him. Klaus stopped them in front of the wolf-skin. "What do you know of the battle at the temple of Lykoplis?"

Dean squinted before touching the wolf-skin. "I never believed those stories."

Smithy howled in the backyard, having joined the pack. Dean's jaw dropped.

"You are . . ."

Klaus nodded. "When the moon is high above the darkened sky, those in the Order of Ophois are free to take its form. By wearing the wolf-skin, you are given a great power. All the strengths of the wolf, no weaknesses of the human."

"I've heard the legends." said Dean, as his jaw dropped. Klaus never cracked a smile.

"It is not only the truth, but the key to the freedom of our people."

"Heil Hitler," Dean said, just above a whisper.

"Indeed, But the Fuhrer is dead. We finish this struggle." Klaus turned to the rest of the Hammer Skins gathered in the living room. "Please, don't fear anything you see."

Klaus pointed towards the back door. Dean took a deep breath, but grinned. He walked toward the backyard. Sonny knew he needed to act now. He put his hand on the cloak.

"Gruppenfuhrer?"

Klaus was surprised and delighted to hear Sonny call him by his rank.

"May I deliver the skin of Ophois to the ritual?"

Klaus gave him a broad smile. "Of course young man. Please have the honor."

Dean walked first to the door. Out the window, he could see the wolves circling the fire-pit. Sonny could smell his sweat nearly drain, sensed his heart beating faster. Dean gripped the door handle. Despite the fear, he turned it.

"All right, boys and girls. We need courage. No matter how strange or frightening this looks, trust me." Dean stood strong.

The door opened. From the back of the line, Sonny watched the Hammer Skins, known as the toughest of the northern Skinheads, walk out into the backyard. One at a time, they gasped or screamed.

Their leader commanded them forward. Klaus used his strength to push from the back of the line. Sonny stared at Klaus, watching his feet as he walked closer to the door. Sonny slipped the cloak under his shirt, neatly fitting it between his skin and the rope tied loosely around his abdomen.

Klaus stepped out onto the back steps, Sonny was thankful for Tom Mansford's paranoid delusions about the Zionist conspiracy as he slammed the back door shut and twisted the deadbolt. Klaus turned, already half-transformed in seconds. He burst through his clothes, his eyes burned a hot red. Sonny took one step back. Klaus slammed on the triple-reinforced glass Tom had installed. It held.

No time to waste. Sonny turned and ran on human legs through the house, smelling the pack running on both sides. He called on the beast as he ran to the front door.

His fur grew. His clothes popped and tore. The ropes pulled taut, and he felt the wolf-skin cloak tight against his chest. He turned the handle with a human hand, and landed a wolf after jumping down the front steps.

He sensed Dana and Chops coming from the left side of the house. Klaus and Murphy had jumped the tall fence. The others barked and held the screaming Hammer Skins in place in the back yard.

Sonny pumped all four legs harder than he ever had. The houses sped past. Behind him he heard Chops and Dana barking.

All the houses lit up as the neighborhood heard the sounds of wild animals in chaos. Klaus jumped and knocked Sonny back, rolling into a the yard of a random neighbor. The front door of the house opened as the two wolves rolled on the ground fighting. A frowzy-looking fat man stood there in flannel pajamas, holding a double-barreled shotgun.

Murphy stood up on his hind legs as a natural wolf couldn't, and barked at the man. The man screamed, unloading both barrels. The large boom echoed miles away.

Murphy yelped as the full blast knocked him back. The

man reloaded as Murphy shook off the shot. But the shot distracted Klaus enough that Sonny slipped out from under him and ran.

Klaus stood up and swung at the man before he could reload the weapon. The old grey Titan among the pack tore the screen door off its hinges, and chopped the man across the head with it three times as though it weighed no more than a swagger stick. Then he neatly folded the door in half and clove the man's skull all the way.

Sonny was down the road, but as fast as he ran, Chops and Dana were after him. Sonny searched the smells for an idea.

He smelled a large sewer drain, then ran over a car that came down the same road. It spun out, knocking back the two wolves in pursuit back. The driver screamed bloody murder.

Sonny loped to the edge of a hill that dropped off thirty feet. At the bottom, a sewer drain spit out something that smelled awful. Industrial or residential waste, it didn't matter. The smell of it was overpowering and unbelievable.

Sonny jumped off the cliff, landing on all fours in the small creek. He slid on moss-covered rocks, and started down the stream. When he got his footing, he ran up into the drain. For a moment or two, he stood there remaining in wolf form.

He couldn't smell the wolves in pursuit anymore, and hoped they couldn't smell him. He found a collection of rocks that had built up during heavy storms, making a little cliff just above the filthy water. It would be a long night, but for now he was safe.

Sonny scratched the rocks, and groomed his feet clean before he curled up to rest.

THIRTY

"The style, all over, it may be different,
But in our hearts, it's all the same."

—Warzone

Klaus cursed the sky, waiting for the moon to rise all day. He had the power to search as a wolf during the daylight, but needed to rest and collect his thoughts. For almost half a century he had protected the skin of Ophois, and in that time he had never lost prey. Of course, he never had to track a member of his own pack.

Last night had not been a good night. They had to eat the Hammer Skins, because they refused to calm down. The neighborhood around Mansford's home went crazy with rumor and speculation about the so-called 'wild and rabid animals,' which the media connected to the North Side attacks.

They had to find the traitor. What was Sonny planning to do with it? *Destroy it or create a rival pack?* Now, for a second night, he searched the city. This time, he choose to search the neighborhood the other skinheads called home. The north side, near the baseball park. They studied a map of areas that Sonny knew well, and split up the areas they thought he might be near his parents, Blue Island or the north side.

Klaus wanted to be alone. He didn't want the new wolves slowing him down. So he waited in a cafe, drinking coffee on Halsted Ave until the moon was high in the sky. It was two days from being full. His powers would be almost at their greatest strength.

He watched two men having coffee. They smiled at

each other a lot. They smelled of attraction. They were homosexuals. He'd sent plenty of those to the ovens as well, and would have sent them all. Now here they were out in the open, everywhere. Another sign of weak American decadence.

One held the hand of the other, before looking over and locking eyes with Klaus, who turned away, disgusted. The two men left quickly, holding hands.

Klaus went to the bathroom. It was time. He looked for a back door to walk out into the alley. He would hide his clothes. Then, when the search was over, if he decided to come back, then he could. Once in the dark alley, Klaus slipped his pants off and unbuttoned his shirt. Then he heard a whisper. If not for his acute hearing he would have missed it.

"My wife knows, sorta. But we're staying together. For the kids, you know."

"Does she think she can cure you, Glen? You can't deny who you are."

Then there was a moan of pleasure. The distinct smell of two men who were sexually excited. Klaus felt his stomach knot in disgust. He took a step forward behind another set of Dumpsters, and saw the two men from the cafe. One had pants at his ankles. The other was on his knees. The man standing up gasped.

"Johnny, stop! Were being wa . . ."

The man on his knees stopped long enough to turn and see naked Klaus.

"You're a little old for me, sweetheart."

Shock and rage shot through Klaus, and he called on the beast. In just a few moments, the bones crunched and shifted. Both men screamed as Klaus's body contorted into wolf form.

Johnny tried to run past the wolf, but Klaus threw him against the brick wall, breaking his back instantly. Glen tried to make his escape. Klaus swung round and dug his claws into his forehead from behind, ripping his scalp free.

Glen fell, screaming and bleeding, to the ground. Klaus picked up Johnny's dying body and held it up in front as he tore at Johnny's flesh with his teeth, eating it as quickly as he could pull it in his mouth.

The rage of it all was too much to handle. Anger over the betrayal and theft, the years in hiding and even the injustice of the Reich falling. He let it out as he tore Johnny apart like a wishbone, then threw the two halves on Glen.

When he'd eaten his fill, Klaus hit all fours and ran out on to the street. Cars screeched to a halt. Klaus barked at them and ran into the night.

***

Smiley was the only skin in the crew considered too young to go drinking. So he sat a alone on the curb at Punkin' Donuts, watching the police cars speed down Belmont towards Halsted just after dark. It wasn't long before units ran up Clark like bats out of hell.

While Smiley observed from the curb, another set of police cars whipped around the corner, going west on Belmont this time. The manager of Dunkin' Donuts who hated all the punks and Skinheads who hung out there stepped out, still holding a steaming mug of coffee.

Smiley, being only twelve years old, received more kindness than most from the Syrian-born Dunkin Donuts manager. Perhaps not this time. "Hey. Little boy . . ." Smiley ignored him. "You got a home to go to?"

Smiley just glared back. The manager pointed with his coffee mug, as cars pulled over to make way for even more cops going west. He had to yell to be heard over the sirens.

"More animal attacks, I just heard on the scanner. Three already tonight."

Smiley nodded and stood up. He wasn't supposed to go back to the drinking alley, but this was big news.

So he ran, pushing his way through the crowd that had gathered to watch the cars speed by. The little skin ran into the darkened alley, and turned into a different, connecting alley under the El tracks. A train rattled over him, heading south. When it was gone, he could hear the laughter and conversation going on in the drinking alley.

They were at the dead end as always, with two cases of beer in three coolers some of the NISH skins had brought with them from Indiana. Smiley didn't see Rooster or Cherry, but he saw Shawna sitting alone on a cooler with her head down. He went to her and tapped her on the shoulder.

She looked up, and her face shifted into an angry stare. "Smiley, how many times do we have to tell you, you're too young . . ."

But the look on his face silenced her. "Something big is happening," Smiley said, in a very calm voice that really wasn't. Everyone stopped suddenly.

Smiley had their attention. One of the NISH skins leaned down in a catcher's stance. "Heard the sirens, little brother. What's going down?"

Smiley took a deep breath. "Manager at Punkin' said animal attacks, all over the North Side."

Shawna froze in shock. Smiley almost shook her. "Just like the thing that killed Marcus," he pointed out.

Shawna didn't say anything. Before Smiley could yell at her to wake up, he heard the growl.

Deep, low like the sound of a Rottweiler gearing up to bark its head off. Smiley could just barely see its reflection in the deep brown of Shawna's eyes. She'd been staring over Smiley's shoulder at the biggest gray wolf she could imagine.

Its belly hung low from feeding. Its breath was quick from running. *And in its eyes, its human eyes, the kilns of Belsen and Buchenwald redlined the dials up, up, up, to ten million, a hundred, a billion . . .*

Beer cans dropped as a bunch of city-slicker skinheads stared at the wolf. Shawna licked her lips. Suddenly, she didn't seem scared, just angry. A kind of anger that Smiley had never seen in his short life.

"Smiley, I need you to drop down and cover your ears."

Smiley dropped. Shawna reached into her flight jacket and pulled out a large revolver as the wolf jumped at her. She fired, and the alley filled with the thunderous sound of the blast. The wolf yelped in pain as the bullet entered its chest.

But the shot didn't slow it down at all. It flattened Shawna, knocking her and the cooler she sat on over. Ice and beer slid across the alley, covering the handgun. The skinheads yelled and screamed as the wolf reared on its hind legs, tearing through them like a sickle through a dry sheaf of wheat.

Smiley stood up. It felt like a baby had its fist in his right ear. He couldn't hear at all on that side.

Faintly, he heard screams. So he imagined glumly that he was probably better off.

The wolf turned, standing up on human-looking legs. Smiley had nothing to fight with. He just chucked the plastic cooler at the beast. It knocked it away harmlessly.

Then the beast grabbed Smiley by his throat. Its snout snapped and moved around unnaturally, like it was speaking. Smiley could just barely hear it, but he had a feeling it was barking loudly.

"Sonny? Where is Sonny?"

Smiley kicked and squirmed uselessly. Shawna screamed, searching through the ice, still unable to find her gun. Smiley spit in the creature's face. It tightened its grip.

His hearing was shot, but Smiley heard the bones in his neck snap as he died.

THIRTY-ONE

"So it's up in the morning,
try to go straight.
Out on the turf,
it's a theater of hate . . ."

—The Toasters

The animal attacks made the national news. Paul couldn't watch any more of it. He knew the truth, and what they were reporting on the news wasn't even close.

He sat in his room, lying on his bed, watching story after story, fuming. The news called it a reign of terror, but it wasn't a rabid wolves as they said. It was monstrous neo-Nazis on a rampage. Try getting Dan Rather to report *that*.

The phone rang. Paul yelled that he had it. Tonight was the night they were supposed to meet Sonny, to hear the second half of his plan. He picked up the cordless, extended the antenna.

Tracy was in tears, and could barely even say hello. Paul listen to her sob through details: Six Skinheads, mostly NISH skinheads, were torn to shreds. Shawna was missing. Then a fresh wave of tears.

Overcome, Tracy couldn't even say the name. "Oh, God, Paul, he was just a little boy. Just a baby . . ."

"Wait. You said the drinking alley, it couldn't be . . .Fuck." Paul punched the wall.

"The bastards killed Smiley," Tracy sobbed. "Just a little boy."

Paul fought back rage, but the tears flowed.

"Come get me," Paul's voice shook. "We sort this fucker tonight."

"But your parents?"

"I don't care. Not now." Paul had planned on just taking off. It didn't matter what trouble he got in.

The reality was that he didn't expect to come home at all. The way some of his Dad's old homies never came home from Direct Actions. or came home in a bag. That didn't matter now.

"Come get me. I'll be ready in twenty minutes."

Paul was about to click the Off button. "Hey, Paulie?"

He waited.

"I love you."

"I love you, too."

He hung up the phone and took a deep breath. His parents were like a lot of Chicago, on their butts in front of the TV, glued to the coverage of the animal attacks. The police hadn't released the details that skinheads were killed, just that a group of young people illegally drinking assaulted in an alley.

Paul walked into the living room. He asked them to turn off the TV. They waited while Paul silently stalled for a minute.

"Dad, you marched with a loaded shotgun, out on the street right?"

Daniel Jackson grinned. He didn't like his son bringing it up.

"Son, the pigs, I mean the police, had just shot our brother Fred, Fred Hampton. We were protecting our families with a show of force because . . ."

"What's your point, Paulie?"

"Mom, you threw Napalm on a sitting senator."

"His campaign was funded by the people who made that napalm," Dad pointed out.

"Your point, Paulie?"

"Look, I don't understand that hair-farmer, hippy-dippy shit you guys were into in the Sixties, but Ma, you were only a year older than me when you chained yourself to a congressman's office door."

His parents didn't say anything so Paul kept going.

"You don't understand my lifestyle, either. I found my

169

cause, and you might not like my shaved head, or how I dress, but I gotta get out there and fight the racists. I gotta fight the bastards, They're different bastards, but the same big struggle. Right?"

"What are you asking?" asked Dad, ignoring the dirty look from Mom.

"For one night, I'm a grown man. Let me make a difference and I'll go to whatever school you want in the fall. Take it seriously." *If I'm alive,* Paul added to himself . . .

***

Paul walked out the front door, Tracy had parked down the street, just in case Paul had to slip out. He stood on the front step and waved her forward. She pulled up, and jumped out of the car. Her face was puffy and red from crying. They hugged. Tracy saw Paul's parents watching from the window.

"Uh, they're letting you go?"

"Yeah, but let's go before they change their mind."

They jumped in the car and took off.

***

The sun dropped behind the city, to the west. The humid summer wind whipped off Lake Michigan on the beach where they were supposed to meet Sonny. Rooster and Cherry had been quiet. No one could quite got over the shock of it all. The goofy playfulness they usually had around each other was gone. Hardly any words were spoken.

It was only then, standing on the beach, looking at the outline rise on the horizon, that Paul realized that the moon was full.

They walked up the beach from the entrance. It was fairly isolated. The traffic on Lake Shore Drive zoomed by above and behind them, but it was almost a mile's walk in from the north or south to this spot.

As they waited, Paul noticed a figure walking toward them from the north. Tracy pointed out someone walking from the direction they came from in the south. "He said he was coming alone," observed Cherry. The sky was taking the purple shade of blackening dusk in the east. The orange of the dipping sun was behind the Chicago skyline.

In the faded light, Sonny became clear to the north, but the person to the south was still a mystery. Sonny approached, wearing a hoodie and Nikes, holding the promised wolf-skin. Tracy reached in her backpack, pulling out a thick, old-looking book.

"Can I see it?" Tracy grabbed the skin, while she flipped through the book. "You said you were coming alone," Rooster pointed out.

"I did. That's Shawna."

"No way!"

Cherry took off, running to her friend. Paul called, trying to get her to wait. No one knew if he told them the truth. The figure was still too far away. Cherry disappeared in the distance.

You could tell they hugged and fell to their knees on the beach. Paul assumed they were crying together. "It's real. The skin of Ophois the Egyptian Wolf-god," Tracy looked up from her book. "The *Pnakotic Manuscipts.* I've been studying it for the last two days."

Rooster got closer, almost in Sonny's face. So what's your plan?"

"We do the ritual," said Sonny. Tracy shook her head.

"You want to start a new pack?"

Sonny nodded. "He is recruiting, bringing skins from other cities. The other night he had a house full of Hammer Skins from Detroit. Next, a crew was supposed to come up from Atlanta. We have to beat them now, before they get stronger. Klaus is powerful. In time, he'll find me. Find this."

Sonny shook the wolf-skin. "Only two things can kill a werewolf, a silver bullet, fired directly into the heart. Or a wound caused by another member of the Order of Ophois."

"I'm in," Paul said and put out his hand for the wolf-skin.

"Oh, no, you're not." Tracy shook her head and gave him a look.

"We have to. This isn't about looking tough, or who can be the most macho skinhead. Not anymore. They killed Marcus, Noah, and Smiley. Do I have to list them all?"

Tracy looked away. Paul pulled her face back and smiled at her, whispering,

"I don't want to do this, but unless you have a secret stash of silver bullets . . ."

"I'm in," Shawna said, limping up to them. In the moonlight, they could see the scars on her face. Four long gashes crossed her beautiful black skin. Her right eye was closed. Judging from the other wounds, it just wasn't there anymore. Tracy and Paul both gasped. Rooster cursed.

Shawna walked up to Sonny, pushing Rooster out of the way. "He was looking for you."

Sonny nodded.

"I watched him," Shawna failed to contain her rage, as her voice built into barking. "I watched him snap a little boy's head off, with his bare hands."

Sonny felt guilt like it squeezed his spine.

"He left me alive so I could give you a message."

"What was it?"

"Fuck that, I ain't his errand girl. You gonna help me kill him? Or does this get ugly?"

THIRTY-TWO

"No one's safe when we march by.
That's why we won't fade and die.
Short hair with braces hanging down.
There'll always be a skinhead in town."

—Combat 84

Sonny unfolded the wolf-skin. The feeling of it in his hands changed, like a switch had been thrown or a key turned in the ignition when he unfolded it. A dull but growing energy pulsed inside it. He felt the pull of the moon on the beast, growing.

Sonny looked around at the group. Rooster and Cherry were nervous, but basically ready. Paul didn't appear to have the fear he did back in the apartment. He was resolved to this path.

Tracy was the most afraid. She put up a shield, had a hard-as-nails look on her face, but Sonny knew better.

"I'll do this. We'll do this. I only have one thing I want an assurance of."

No one said anything. What could they say?

"Right, I'll perform the ritual for everyone but Tracy."

"No," Tracy shook her head. "Don't start this now. This can't be about us."

"I ain't gonna do it, Trace. I still love you. It's not about that, I want you and Paul to be happy. If we don't make it back, I need you to keep the cloak, bury it or destroy it, whatever."

Tracy's heartbeat and blood flow relaxed. Paul went up behind her and put his arms on her shoulders. "It's a good idea."

"Shouldn't I have a say in this?" Tracy insisted.

173

"It's your call, Trace," Sonny grinned. "but, someone needs to stay here and keep an eye on our clothes."

"Okay." Tracy nodded. Paul shrugged, looking confused. "We're getting naked?"

Sonny laughed

"Unless you want to lose that gear forever. You're going to outgrow your clothes quick."

***

Paul unlaced his Docs and stared at Tracy. She wrapped herself in his bomber jacket and sat on the beach. Cherry and Rooster were already out of their Docs.

Paul looked away as Cherry pushed her jeans down. He wanted to look at her long, tattooed legs but didn't want Rooster or Tracy to catch him looking. As soon as the the first Doc Marten was untied, he slid it off his foot, still having to wrench it a bit.

He held the boot in his hand, staring at it. Even after a mile of walking in the sand, parts of the leather were still shined to perfection. Nervous energy and weeks of being grounded gave him plenty of time to work on his shine. A few months ago a pair of Doc Marten boots were nothing more than wish, something to make him feel like a real big city skin.

"Doesn't seem right, does it?" Sonny asked.

Paul looked up at him. "Excuse me?"

"Doesn't seem right, a Skinhead going to battle without his boots."

Paul looked at his own reflection in the boot. This summer changed him. He was embarrassed just thinking of that wanna-be fresh cut that stepped onto Belmont two months ago.

"I don't know man. Boots, that's just uniform." Paul grinned. "Seems to me the most important thing a skinhead brings to the battle is his heart."

Sonny nodded, stepping away.

"Hey, Sonny."

Sonny stopped.

"Speaking of heart, Trace says you have a good heart. I, for one, find that hard to believe."

"You want to know how it happened? Being a Nazi?" Sonny nervously kicked at the sand.

"Yeah, curious." Paul stared at him waiting for an answer.

"When I'm honest with myself, I can admit that there just wasn't enough anger here for me to belong." Sonny walked to the circle that formed.

Paul was the last to take off his pants and nervously walk toward the circle. Rooster was on Paul's right, Sonny just past them. Sonny choose Rooster first, he stood in front of him.

"This is gonna hurt, at first."

Rooster nodded.

Sonny's voice grew strange. "When the moon is high above the darkened sky, those in the Order of Ophois are free to take its form. By wearing the wolf-skin, you are given a great power. All the strengths of the wolf, no weaknesses of the human."

Sonny held out the cloak. Rooster gave Cherry a long look. She smiled. "Right behind you, baby."

Rooster took the cloak in his hands, swinging it over his back. The cloak covered him completely.

Under it, Rooster grunted and screamed. Cherry closed her eyes. Sonny stepped back. Paul couldn't watch.

"When he's done, pass it around."

Tracy sat back from the circle. Paul heard her gasp from behind him and opened his eyes. Sonny extended his arms, and let the fur grow out. He dropped to all fours. The bones throughout his body snapped, popped and moved under his skin. His face contorted, the skin bubbling and running like cheese. This time, Paul couldn't turn away.

What the fuck are we doing? But part of him knew they didn't have a choice. In just a few moments, Sonny stood on four legs.

They'd almost forgotten about Rooster. The cloak shook off him, and the Sharp was gnashing terrible teeth, experimentally flexing guitar-pick claws and grinning like a mutt on a hot day. An unnaturally large wolf-mutt, the size of a mastiff or a small horse, covered in muscles that popped under the thick fur. Rooster bared his new rack of teeth. In the moonlight, they gleamed.

The Rooster-wolf took careful steps on the sand before lifting its head to the moon. For the first time since he saw the boneheads change their skins, Paul felt the fear drain away. They'd lived the last two days in fear, but now the tide had turned.

It didn't matter what he had to endure physically. This was about his crew. They had fight together to stop these monsters.

Sonny walked up to Rooster. The wolves nuzzled, communicating in language beyond the human observer. Sonny pointed his snout, and they ran through the opening in the circle. Picking up speed and soon were circling them. Like a pit. Like a mosh.

Tracy called out. "It's part of the ritual. The wolves circle, until the pack is newly formed."

Cherry walked to the center to pick up the cloak, flipped it around and covered herself. Almost immediately, she screamed and grunted, as Rooster had done.

It sounded as if she were dying under the skin. This only lasted a few moments, but to Paul it seemed like forever.

Then Cherry threw the cloak off. The transformation was only half-complete. Cherry lay on her back, hair still growing out into fur just as her arms and legs twisted into shape. She spun on the sand and stood, finally a vicious-looking wolf with the same jade eyes she'd always had, beautiful in her wrath.

Rooster and Sonny howled up at the moon, Cherry responded with angry barks as she ran beyond Paul and Shawna to be with her mate. Paul closed his eyes, listening to the wolves running behind him in the sand. He tried to imagine himself there, as one of them.

He was afraid, but thought of the victims, Smiley most of all. No matter what it took, they had to be stopped.

Shawna stepped forward already, but Paul jumped at the

cloak and swung it over his shoulder. It was like suddenly being in a tent. Humid air encased him, like the cloak was shrink-wrapped to his skin.

Paul's skin was boiling. Every bone in his body was taking a drywall screw from an uncaring electric screwdriver at the same time. He screamed . . . but then Pain transmuted to Pleasure as the joints locked into new places.

Fur sprouted all along his body. Muscles formed that he had never felt before. His teeth elongated to sharpened points and his face changed, slung into a snout. He was being twisted, put through a shredder, a scream building without a voice box that could properly form the sound.

When he opened his mouth to scream, he felt a sudden calm instead. The pain was over. He felt the earth under four strong legs. Paul shook off the cloak, and looked to the moon. To Mother Moon.

Amazing power surged between him and the white ball in the sky.

He turned his new face to the sky, and the sound of the howl built in his belly until he let it go into the night. His fur-covered ears followed the sound as it bounced across the land for miles. His senses came awake. He could smell Tracy across the fire pit. Feel her heart beating faster. He knew he had to run.

THIRTY-THREE

"All you punks and all you Teds,
National Front and natty dreads,
Mods, rockers, hippies and Skinheads,
Keep on fighting 'til you're dead . . ."

—The Specials

The moon pushed Paul forward. He ran down the beach, chasing the others at a speed he never thought he would travel on foot. Of course, he never expected to have feet like this.

When they hit the grass just past the end of the beach, they surged forward. He could smell his friends even when he didn't see them, and knew where they were without looking. Each had their own scent. The night was alive in a way Paul never could have guessed.

Sonny was the pack leader, having the most experience. They had a lot riding on the plan, and only hoped that Klaus was predictable. They didn't waste time running along the sidewalk up Belmont Avenue. There was almost a mile to travel before they got to Punkin' Donuts.

They passed a couple walking a yappy little ankle-biter dog. The couple jumped out of the way screaming, and the dog barked wildly. ff in the distance, several miles away, a faint howl echoed in the night. Sonny stopped and his ears perked up to listen.

Another howl sounded off, a few miles to the north of the last one. A third, closer, just west of Punkin.' Sonny turned back to the pack and looked at them.

He couldn't speak, of course, but Paul understood he was warning them that the rival crew knew they were coming. Sonny pushed off with his back legs, running even faster.

178

Paul had to really work his new legs to catch up.

It was all so surreal, like he was behind a movie camera zooming along the sidewalk. Cars filled the streets like normal, but the sidewalks were empty. He knew the city was afraid of animal attacks. Cars honked, and people screamed as they rolled up their windows. Paul could see the corner on Clark, smell the rank overpowering smell of the Dunkin' Donuts belching out.

The parking lot was empty. That was strange. Sonny, Cherry and Rooster jumped over cars stopped at the traffic light on Clark, and into the lot. They circled, Sonny howling an intense warcry that rattled the glass panes on the donut shop.

Paul was about to jump over a car, when he felt something hit him. He smelled the wolf, but too late. They both rolled into cars parked on the street, banging into the side door of the last one they hit. Shawna jumped on top of the attacking wolf and savagely bit down.

The people in the cars watching them yelled, and screamed. Shawna bit down harder on the wolf's neck. Bones snapped as Shawna used her wolf-mouth to throw the beast in the air.

The light turned green, and the first car peeled forward. The attacking wolf hit the front windshield. The car carried the wolf half-way across Belmont before it slid dead into the road.

***

Sonny had smelled Dana coming fast from the south on Clark. He got there just in time to see Shawna throw her up on to the car speeding across Belmont. That wasn't what killed her. It was the bite.

Dana's wolf-body convulsed on the ground. The cars swerved to avoid her. Finally, one stopped to look, but despite the heat of the summer night the gawker kept his window up.

Dana whimpered as a wolf, but her body continued to shift in the middle of the street. The fur fell out on the pavement like a Christmas tree shedding pine needles. The slight, warm breeze picked up the fur and spun it in the air.

Her face contorted back to a bruised version of her human visage. The bones cracked and snapped, but this time no healing came. She felt the full pain of the transformation.

Dana gave one last cry as a woman before her body stopped. When Dana died, she had one human hand, one hairless wolf paw.

Two new smells came to Sonny. Ace and Rachel raced toward them. Sonny gave a short howl and his pack followed behind him as he ran to the drinking alley. Police would come. He didn't want to risk anymore innocent life.

The pack ran through one alley and into the second alley where the skins gathered to drink. Tonight, it was empty. In the distance, Sonny could hear trains rattling their way closer from both the north and the south.

Ace and Rachel entered the alley slowly. A mile to the west, another wolf howled out. The sound was closer than last time, but still faint over the distance. The reinforcements were letting them know they were on the way.

Another howl, even closer, a wolf coming from the north. In the wake of the attacks, the sound of howling wolves must have rattled people's nerves everywhere around the North Side. The two Nazi werewolves took careful steps around the corner.

Ace snarled and barked at Sonny. Rooster stepped forward. The north-bound El sped up the tracks above them, shaking the whole world.

Ace took off running, Rooster jumped forward. The two wolves tangled and twisted, biting at each other. Rachel ran around them. Cherry opened her mouthful of razor-sharp teeth and jumped at Rachel. The two wolves spun in mid-air, but landed with Cherry gripping Rachel in her jaws like an exuberantly teething pit-bull pup who just wants to grip . . . and chew . . .and grip harder. Cherry bit downas the train moved north and silence returned to the alley. Everyone could hear the bones breaking in Rachel's neck.

Sonny stopped for a moment to watch Cherry. She was

a natural. The fists-and-boots Skinbird in her came out all the way the instant she threw off the cloak. Cherry picked up Rachel in those Jaws Of Life again, twisted . . . and then flipped her into the nearest Dumpster, as though she weighed no more than a Kleenex. *Dong, Dong.* It sounded like a giant gong.

Sonny turned back when Paul and Shawna ran at Ace. Rooster screamed in a human voice. The sounds of his bones snapping and popping made a ugly harmony with the the screams. He'd half reverted to human form while still locked in Ace's jaw.

Rooster was bleeding out on the pavement. Paul jumped, knocking into Ace's midsection. Ace let go of Rooster and spun out on the ground. Cherry looked up at Rooster. He shook and bled out, naked on the ground. He rolled over and with his dying breath he whispered.

"Cherry."

Rooster rolled on his back as the fur fell out. His body slumped on the ground, as just behind them, Ace tried to duck out, scampering backward.

Cherry howled like the sirens of Los Alamos, cutting off his path before he righted himself in the alley and jumped on him, tearing at his flesh. *Cherry-Baby was still teething. But Ace could help with that . . .*

Ace howled in agony, Sonny couldn't see what was happening under Cherry, but he saw the muscles in her wolf-back working. Faintly, under the fur, he could see the the tattoo of the eagle that in human form went shoulder-to-shoulder.

Ace's voice cracked like a needle skipping on a record, and suddenly his howl lugged down into the screams of a human begging for mercy. "No, please, God, NO!!!"

Cherry jumped free. Ace was ripped up like Shredded Wheat. She bounced over to Rooster's body and licked his face. Rooster didn't move. Paul and Shawna circled his body. There was a low growl building in Cherry's throat.

It shocked Sonny when Cherry lifted her head and howled a deep, angry howl at the moon. The southbound train rattled over them, and still he could hear the agony in her voice.

In all the excitement Sonny hadn't noticed as Murphy and Smithy entered the alley. By now they had to have smelled Ace and Rachel's dead bodies. They were still around the corner, out of sight, but walking slowly toward them. Sonny ran to each member of his pack and nudged them, letting them know to pay attention.

The SHARP wolves walked around until they were in formation, with Sonny out front. Sonny was panting like a dog, worried he'd already worn himself out, when he smelled another smell. Older, stronger.

Klaus Schroeder stepped into the alley. Now, it was on. For good or bad, it would end it here tonight.

THIRTY-FOUR

"Please don't ask me.
I will refuse . . ."

—Pailhead

Murphy and Smithy turned the corner into the drinking alley. Sonny kicked his back legs, smelling Klaus right behind him. Klaus turned the corner standing up, fully dressed and human. Paul and Cherry shared a look. Sonny stepped in front of her, urging her to wait.

"He just saved your life, young lady." Klaus grinned. "I ran the forests of Germany under the full moon a lifetime before you were born."

Murphy stepped forward, ready to attack. Klaus put up his hand, signaling him to wait. "Now, now, my friend. Let's have a short talk first. We might be able to avoid further bloodshed."

Cherry barked.

"My, my you are a feisty one." Klaus took a step forward. "Where is it, Sonny? The Skin of Ophois?"

Shawna ran forward, barking viciously. Klaus grinned, letting his arm transform. Shawna jumped at him, but Klaus held her in the air by her neck. His muscled arms had grown wolf-fur, his hands deadly claws cutting into her neck. She whimpered like a dog trying to run at the end of a chain.

"Give me the cloak, walk away, and I'll declare a truce."

Cherry and Paul snarled. Murphy and Smithy snarled back at them. Sonny stood on his hind legs, controlling them enough to grow back to human length. The rest of his body remained wolf. Klaus seemed surprised by the control displayed. Sonny stepped forward.

183

Klaus pulled Shawna closer, sniffing her fur. "A nigger doesn't deserve this gift."

He squeezed, breaking Shawna's neck instantly. Cherry and Sonny both ran forward. Klaus threw Shawna's body at them, knocking them back.

"Never mind. I can smell it on all you, I know where it is and who holds it still." Klaus snapped his still-human fingers. "Kill them."

Murphy and Smithy ran forward. Klaus dropped back, taking off running through the alley. He remained in human form, but ran faster than any normal man of his age. Sonny pushed Shawna's body off in time to see Murphy jump at him. Sonny used his half-human claw to smack the wolf, sending him into a brick wall.

Smithy ran fast at Paul . . .

***

Paul watched the wolf run at him. Somehow, deep inside, he knew that this was the guy he kicked in the face during his first fight. Sonny said his name was Smithy. Now he was a bloodthirsty wolf, drooling because he wanted to hurt Paul so badly.

Paul held still, only moving at the last moment. Smithy slammed into the chain-link fence behind Paul. Past that, Smithy was so busy attempting to stand that he didn't sense the claw before it slashed his face.

Paul ran at him full-steam. Smithy howled in anger as Paul slammed his face into his enemy's stomach. Paul let his fangs grow sharper in his mouth, letting his body respond to the attack. He ripped and tore away at Smithy's skin.

Paul kept biting. Smithy howled. The tearing continued, until the painful howling changed to the voice of a man, as Ace's voice had changed back when Cherry dispatched him.

Paul saw a naked young man, his guts torn and pulled out. He stepped back in disgust and sorrow. Something turned in his stomach. Paul looked at the torn guts in Smithy's dying ribcage. Everything in his stomach rushed to the surface.

Smithy spit blood. "Nigger half-breed pig."

Paul felt his form shifting. He rolled on the ground, vomiting up something large and chunky before his body snapped and cracked back into naked human form. He rolled over and looked at Smithy.

"I was just starting to feel sorry for you."

Smithy tried to crawl forward, but his body fell apart even further sending off torrents of pain. He yelped. "Porch-monkey coon . . ." Smithy collapsed fighting for a single breath.

Paul rolled away with his back to Smithy.

"Your last words. Really?"

***

Sonny stood on human legs, gripping the fully wolf form of Murphy by his neck. Cherry barked behind him. Sonny swung Murphy's whole body into the brick wall at the edge of the alley.

Murphy howled, snarled and fought. It was too late. Sonny had his claws deep into his skin, and bashed him against into the stone. Bones all through Murphy's body crunched and snapped.

He could hear Smithy begging for his life behind him, but Sonny locked up with Murphy's burning red eyes. With an intense war cry, Sonny slammed Murphy into the wall, and the fur on his body rained onto the ground. Murphy's human form fought to reassert itself, but his body had already shut down. It looked pathetic, a naked wolf free of its fur, a half human face twisted in transformation.

"You . . ." Murphy tried to speak but his body was trapped between forms. "Fucking race traitor . . ."

Sonny threw his body to the ground, Murphy cried out in pain but his body didn't shift anymore. He just slowly died.

185

***

Paul rolled around on the dirty pavement in the alley. Too exhausted to even get his arms out from under him, he looked at the older man's twisted and tortured body.

"Fuck!" said Paul. He used a Dumpster to prop himself up, and cursed again, looking at Rooster and Shawna's bodies. Cherry seemed in perfect control as she shifted back to her human form. This time Paul couldn't take his eyes off her sweat-slicked, white-skinned,tattooed body. She was leaning over on all fours but stood up, heaving her decorated breasts with deep breaths. Her lips and chin were covered in blood.

"Don't you fuckin' stare at me!"

Paul turned away quickly, but felt the blood on his own chin. Sonny stood still in mostly wolf-form with his back to Paul.

"Sonny?"

Sonny turned and growled. Paul wiped the blood off his mouth onto his arm. "We need to re-group and talk."

Sonny's body seemed to relax. The fur sucked into his skin and he fell on to all fours, exhausted.

"We don't have time for this."

Cherry leaned over Rooster, rubbing his face gently. She took in long deep breaths. Rage, sorrow and exhaustion lurked below the surface.

"Bullshit." She was masking sorrow with rage. "We got them on the ropes."

Sonny shook his head. "Klaus is the most powerful one."

Paul put his hands on his bald head. "Did you hear him? He knows Tracy has the cloak."

"What?" Sonny looked at Paul.

"I know where it is and who holds it," Paul walked back toward the street. "He said that, right before he took off like Carl fucking Lewis."

Paul reached out with his new wolf-senses, smelling the old man. He was moving fast toward the lake shore. Paul looked up at the train track. A northbound train rumbled down the track, but the moonlight shone between the tracks into the alley.

"Give me the strength," Paul whispered up at the Moon. The train came closer, and the tracks shook. It felt like the whole earth did when they came through. The moon answered silently.

Paul felt an energy growing inside him, not a second wind but probably a sixth by that point. He closed his eyes as the fur came shooting out, dropping to his knees as the train rolled above. His bones shifted and popped under his skin. By the time the train moved on, he was a wolf again.

Cherry leaned down and kissed Rooster on the forehead. "Goodbye sweetheart. I'm going kill every fucking Nazi I can get my hands on, for you."

She squeezed his hand tight as the fur cascaded from her skin. She only let go when her hands turned into claws, then ran instantly to Paul's side. They took off down the alley. Sonny ran the alley as a human but jumped out on to Belmont avenue as a wolf.

THIRTY-FIVE

"You can't see beyond your nose.
What's making you so blind?"

—Agnostic Front

Tracy moved over to the fire-pit where they had the memorial party for Marcus. She feared they were going to have a few more of those before she left for college. The firewood was set up there. She reached into Cherry's jeans and found a pack of Marlboro Lights and a lighter. She used a couple of pieces of paper and the lighter to start the fire.

It burned for four minutes before the howling started. It was far-off, but she knew what it meant. She was bored, scared and worried. She sat with the wolf skin on her lap and shivered when she heard the sound of howls increasing. They were getting insistent, and closer.

The skin of Ophois suddenly felt warm in her lap. She felt a pulsing heat on her legs. It made her uncomfortable, so she pulled her backpack over and buried deep inside the bag filled with dirty laundry she'd piled up while staying with Rooster and Cherry.

The howls got closer with each minute. Cars honked around the north-side, creating a certain rhythm.

What if they're coming for me? I shouldn't have stayed here alone . . .

The continued chorus of noises traveled closer like wave across a lake, and made Tracy nervous. She never smoked. She needed to do something with her hands, to calm down. She picked up Cherry's cigarettes,put one awkwardly in her mouth and lit it.

It was like the smoke entered he lungs and started to

punch. Tracy coughed and threw the damn thing in the fire. She was still hacking when she heard the voice.

"Might I have one of those?" Tracy jumped and turned at the voice. She relaxed when she saw the old man. He was tall, but awkwardly dressed in khakis and a golf shirt. He wore a paper-boy's hat, but she assumed it was just the hat the old man owned. The old man smiled. His face was well lit by the fire.

"Help yourself," Tracy handed him the pack and the lighter.

The old man sat on one of the stumps that had been drawn up by the fire. He motioned to the one near him and Tracy sat down. The old man held the flame to the cigarette and breathed in deeply and effortlessly blew the smoke out.

He seemed relaxed. It helped put Tracy at ease, even though the howling of the wolves got more intense in the distance.

"I could use the company." Tracy smiled.

"I was surprised to see a young woman out here all by herself." His words sounded awkward.

"I'm waiting for some friends," Tracy said nervously.

The wolves howled again, closer but still some distance away.

"I'm sure they will be here soon." The old man said with a little accent coming through.

Tracy stared at the fire, then back at the old man. She welcomed company at first but now the guy was creeping her out. She needed to break the ice.

"I'm Tracy, and you are?"

The old man dragged deeply on the cigarette, it's red cherry glowed and as he sucked in the smoke.

"It's been a long time since I had a cigarette."

"I don't smoke as you could probably tell," Tracy smiled. The old man didn't smile. He leaned in a little closer.

"I haven't smoked since Auschwitz." He took a shorter drag, and blew out the smoke. He spoke in a perfect German accent. "It's amazing but it takes me right back."

Tracy's jaw dropped. She stared across the fire at the old

189

man, and felt suddenly stupid. It was Klaus Schroeder. In the distance the wolves howled. That was probably her friends. They were probably entering the beach, still a mile away.

"It's not just the smells and feeling of a place, but that power. You can't imagine what it felt like to be a commander in the Reich."

Tracy kept her eyes locked with Klaus, but her mind was on the wolf-skin in her backpack behind her. "I know it's behind you," Klaus said matter-of-factly.

"What is?" Tracy faked innocence.

Klaus threw the cigarette into the fire. "Enough games. Give it to me or I'll take it. Simple."

The howling grew intense, coming down the beach like police sirens. Klaus stood up. Tracy kicked the burning logs with her Docs. Klaus screamed in anger.

Tracy picked up the backpack and ran down the beach, turning to see the wolf-man standing on human legs. Klaus barked. Tracy reached into her backpack and searched, praying that her research had been correct . . .

THIRTY-SIX

"We will never say die in our city,
Never say die in our streets . . ."

—Angelic Upstarts

Paul manged to find an extra gear inside him, and pulled ahead of Sonny and Cherry. They ran as fast as they could across the beach. In the distance they were drawn to the fire. They could smell Tracy, but they could also smell Klaus at the fire. They were both still for a excruciatingly long minute.

Just beyond his bouncing vision, Paul saw the fire burst into the air. Tracy took off in a run. She couldn't outrun Klaus. She was only seconds from death. Paul ran and jumped far too soon, missing Klaus, landing in the fire and rolling out into the legs of the older werewolf. Klaus turned to attack Paul, and Cherry jumped into the air jaws open wide.

Klaus swatted her out of the air like a fly. She landed on the beach, rolled around and got back up, staring at the powerful wolf, trying to think of an attack. Sonny went after Klaus. They ran at each other, claws slashing.

Klaus shifted his right hand back to a human hand, and grabbed Sonny by a tuft of fur. He twisted him around, shoving him face-down into the sand. Cherry came at him again, but he just knocked her out of the way.

Paul jumped at Klaus, who knocked him back, Paul lost control and felt his human form reasserting itself. Paul crawled backwards on the beach, feeling his human form returning, hearing his own voice was a shock. *"No, no, fuck . . ."*

It was useless. The fur went back into his skin. He felt sand sticking to his bare, sweaty back. Klaus stomped towards him as a wolf, standing straight up, ready to tear him apart. Paul

191

backed up towards Tracy. She was pulling stuff out of her backpack, throwing it on the beach.

Klaus reached down for Paul, seconds from picking the young man like a weed, when Sonny jumped on the older wolf's back. Sonny's wolf teeth bit into his neck, but Klaus shook fighting to get him off.

Paul reached Tracy. As she pulled a revolver out of her backpack. Paul looked at her, surprised. She unfolded the wolf-skin of Ophois and a silver bullet rolled out into her hand.

"I hope it was long enough."

Paul turned back in time to see Klaus flex his shoulders and his arms wide, before throwing Sonny a good distance. Klaus turned back and roared at them. Tracy pushed the bullet into the gun and spun it until it was ready to go. Klaus moved closer. She pulled the hammer back, and roared"Follow your Leader!"

Klaus was on top of her. Tracy shoved the gun into his chest and pulled the trigger. Klaus screamed as parts of his heart and lungs blew out his back.

Wolf's blood splattered on her face before Tracy fell back into Paul's arms. Wolf fur was next to rain on them, sticking to the sweat and blood. It was itchy and they both tried to shake it off.

The old wolf stepped back, his fur falling out. Suddenly Klaus tensed again. Paul cringed at the sound of something squishing inside of the older wolf. A hand broke through Klaus Schroeder's chest holding his damaged heart.

With a partially human arm still pierced through his chest, the wolf transformed back into human form. He gasped and screamed as his bones creaked and snapped. He let out a horrible scream as the reality of his human form came back around him. Klaus wanted to curse, but life drained out of him.

Cherry used her foot push the old dead man off her arm, and onto the beach with a thud. She turned and pitched his beating heart into the fire.

"I need a cigarette."

Paul looked at Tracy, they were both covered in blood but hugged each other tight.

"Where'd you get a silver bullet?"

Tracy grinned over his shoulder. "Big city, yellow pages."

Paul laughed.

"Finding it wasn't the hard part. It was it was supposed to be in the skin during an entire night of the full moon to work."

Paul looked back to see Cherry. She stood naked over the fire, watching Klaus Schroeder's heart sizzle into ash. Tracy looked around. Paul knew what she was looking for.

Where was everybody else?

Paul cringed.

"It's just us and . . ."

Paul looked around. Sonny was gone. Paul stood up but he could smell his scent, and he was charging off to the north, already a half a mile away.

THIRTY-SEVEN

"The blood, the honor, the truth.
I thought it would never end."

—Agnostic Front

Spring was finally here. After a long winter, 1990 turned
out to be a warmer-than-average spring in Southern Illinois.
Tracy'd been placed in a dorm on the edge of campus, near
a small wooded area, and spent the year hard at work on her
studies. She went to a few parties, and went drinking with
some of the Punk women she met at school, but the attention
from guys was getting grating.

She told them she was seeing someone. But if he wasn't
around, and worse, a six-hour drive away, it was like he didn't
exist. Tracy took the train home for weekends when she
could, talked to him on the phone for a least a few minutes
every day, but it wasn't the same.

The events of the past summer came up in nightmares,
mostly ones that relived all the funerals they attended.
Rooster was buried in Northern Indiana. His parents didn't
like Cherry, and tried to keep her from being involved. He
had no living will (what twenty-six-year-old does?). In the
end they let her speak to the crowd.

His parents didn't like it at first when all the skinheads
piled into the church. Cherry did an excellent of summing up
the man that Rooster (or, as they knew him, Richard) was.

Shawna only knew Skinheads in the states, so she had a
moving service where she liked to party and not too far from
where she died: in the drinking alley. Her dad took her and
Marcus back to be buried in England. That seemed fitting to
everyone.

Smiley's funeral was hard on everyone. Except his mother, who was a bigger drunk than anyone knew. She spiraled downward after his father died. That was the most heart-breaking of all the funerals for everyone except Tracy.

She and Paul were the only ones who went to Sonny's funeral. His parents, sister and a extended family were there. His mother gave a Tracy a 'How dare you' stare, but never said a word. Tracy had to come home from college for that one.

Sonny's body was never found. He was reported missing. With all the dead skinheads found around Chicago that summer, his family assumed the worst. It was somewhere around October when they decided to say goodbye.

It was impossible not to re-live it all, on a day like today. The harsh cold of winter was gone, and the warmth of summer was just coming back to the air. School would be out soon, and she'd have to face that world again.

Tracy held the two books she needed for her afternoon classes under her arms, walking a path that cut through woods on campus, back towards her dorm.

She stopped when she heard footsteps, leaves crunching and a branch breaking. No movement in the woods, but a bird sang a song. She took a few more steps, and then she heard it again. Tracy turned towards the woods and stared into the tree line. She heard heavy breathing. A dog was behind her. A large one. She turned around slowly to look at it.

She relaxed when she saw the wolf. The wolf sat on its hind legs, and looked at her.

"Sonny?"

He always struggled to belong, never quite fit in with punks, SHARPS, it didn't matter. That night walking up to Rooster's apartment when she asked him what it felt like, to be a wolf he said "Home."

He whispered it of course and when she asked him to repeat that he grinned and refused.

"You home, Sonny?"

The wolf responded by running up to her leg. Her heart beat a little faster as the animal rubbed its soft fur against her, looked up with a jovial expression, then took off back into the woods.

EPILOGUE

"Boot boys. Boot boys.
Staying alive.
Boot boys, Boot boys.
Don't ever die . . ."

—Infa-Riot

Paul walked out of the Belmont El station, into the busy Friday evening rush of people. He skipped last-period PE to drop off his books and get some grub before heading up north.

He kept his promise with his parents and hit the books. He needed to turn his grades around if he was going to follow Tracy to school. His parents sensed a change in him, a confidence for sure, but honestly they had no idea. No one did except Tracy, Cherry and himself. Who would believe him anyways?

Cherry was a natural. Paul got the feeling she was always part wolf. She'd made Nazi hunting into an art form. They'd accepted a truth about themselves: If you're going to be monster, you might as well do something positive. Like hunting larger monsters, to keep from becoming less of one yourself.

She also helped Paul learn to control the power. He looked a little bigger. Everyone assumed he hit the weights. Suddenly he was an elder, as the Chicago skinhead scene had a major turn-over between '89 and '90.

Paul was almost to Punkin' Donuts when he saw a young kid walking into the store The Alley. Paul stopped at the Alley's edge, and got a good look at the kid. He was older than Smiley was, but not by much.

He had on a pair of crappy combat boots that were so big on his feet they looked like clown shoes. His father probably passed those down. He had on suspenders that were thick as rulers, and his young head was shaved down almost to the skull. He wore imitation bomber jacket that looked ridiculous.

Paul laughed, wondering if he looked this green the first time Tracy saw him walk into the same store to shop for Doc Martens. Paul followed him into the store. The kid went straight for the black ten-holed Docs.

Paul walked up behind the kid. "Nice pair of boots."

The kid smiled, his eyes still on them. "Yeah, I don't have enough money."

"You from here in Chicago?"

The kid turned around and looked at Paul but didn't say a word. That's when Paul saw the Confederate Flag stitched on the sleeve of the jacket. Paul shrugged. "You serious, kid?"

He just stared at Paul. The kid was tiny compared to him, and he didn't know what to do. Paul laughed.

"Relax, man, I don't want to fight."

The young kid put the boot down, but he still looked like a ball of tension.

"Why you want to be Nazi?"

The kid tried to walk past him. Paul grabbed and held him tightly by the arm.

"I've seen it before. You got a lot of anger, but that is no way to make friends, or get revenge."

The kid tried to pull his arm free. He couldn't. "Let go of me."

"Nah." Paul shook his head. "I'm the nice one that will help you pull that patch off your arm and teach you how to be a *real* skinhead."

Paul pulled him in closer. One of the employees of the store walked over and asked if there was trouble. Paul whispered into the Nazi kid's ear.

"Perhaps you heard of my friend Cherry. She's the mean one that'll rip your fucking head off."

Paul let go, and the kid ran toward the door.

"Keep your eye out for Cherry. I warned you."

The woman working the store hung out at Punkin' sometimes. She gave Paul a dirty look.

"Hey I didn't hurt a hair on his head." Paul smiled.

"He doesn't have any." She wasn't laughing.

Paul grinned, walking outside. The moon was coming up over the horizon. Not quite full, but in another day or so. The Nazi kid stopped at the end of the alley. Over the sounds of the city a wolf howled at the rising moon.

The Nazi took off towards the El station like a sprinter. Maybe he'd heard the legends about Cherry. They didn't stand a chance.

DAVID AGRANOFF is the author the Wonderland award nominated short story collection *Screams From A Dying World* (Best collection 2009), and two previously published novels *The Vegan Revolution...with Zombies* and *Hunting the Moon Tribe*. A cross-genre tribute to both kung-fu and horror movies the Wuxia style Chinese dark fantasy *Hunting the Moon Tribe* began life as screenplay that was a finalist in several amateur screen-writing competitions including the prestigious Nicholl Fellowship in 2004. His short fiction has appeared in the Magazine of Bizarro fiction, Nameless Journal and Dark Discoveries. His short story "Punkupine Moshers of the Apocalypse" appeared in *The Best Bizarro Fiction of the Decade* published in 2012.

Agranoff grew up in Bloomington Indiana but has lived in Dayton, Ohio, Syracuse New York, San Diego, California, Port Angeles Washington and Portland Oregon. He is a Rabbit Dad, but also has a cat named Asimov. He credits late night television for who he grew up to be. Sammy Terry and Black Belt theater on Friday nights and Headbanger's ball on Saturdays. His first punk record was the Dead Kennedys and he thought is funny that they used the F word.

Agranoff was vocalist of a skinhead hardcore Stand Alone when he was 16 years old. They wrote 15 songs played 5 shows and never recorded anything.

www.DavidAgranoff.blogspot.com

deadite
press

"Urban Gothic" Brian Keene - When their car broke down in a dangerous inner-city neighborhood, Kerri and her friends thought they would find shelter inside an old, dark row home. They thought they would be safe there until help arrived. They were wrong. The residents who live down in the cellar and the tunnels beneath the city are far more dangerous than the streets outside, and they have a very special way of dealing with trespassers. Trapped in a world of darkness, populated by obscene abominations, they will have to fight back if they ever want to see the sun again.

"Ghoul" Brian Keene - There is something in the local cemetery that comes out at night. Something that is unearthing corpses and killing people. It's the summer of 1984 and Timmy and his friends are looking forward to no school, comic books, and adventure. But instead they will be fighting for their lives. The ghoul has smelled their blood and it is after them. But that's not the only monster they will face this summer . . . From award-winning horror master Brian Keene comes a novel of monsters, murder, and the loss of innocence.

"Clickers" J. F. Gonzalez and Mark Williams- They are the Clickers, giant venomous blood-thirsty crabs from the depths of the sea. The only warning to their rampage of dismemberment and death is the terrible clicking of their claws. But these monsters aren't merely here to ravage and pillage. They are being driven onto land by fear. Something is hunting the Clickers. Something ancient and without mercy. *Clickers* is J. F. Gonzalez and Mark Williams' gore-soaked cult classic tribute to the giant monster B-movies of yesteryear.

"Clickers II" J. F. Gonzalez and Brian Keene- Thousands of Clickers swarm across the entire nation and march inland, slaughtering anyone and anything they come across. But this time the Clickers aren't blindly rushing onto land - they are being led by an intelligence older than civilization itself. A force that wants to take dry land away from the mammals. Those left alive soon realize that they must do everything and anything they can to protect humanity – no matter the cost. *This isn't war, this is extermination.*

"The Book of a Thousand Sins" Wrath James White - Welcome to a world of Zombie nymphomaniacs, psychopathic deities, voodoo surgery, and murderous priests. Where mutilation sex clubs are in vogue and torture machines are sex toys. No one makes it out alive – not even God himself.
"If Wrath James White doesn't make you cringe, you must be riding in the wrong end of a hearse."
    -Jack Ketchum

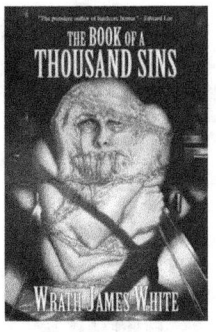

"Whargoul" Dave Brockie - It is a beast born in bullets and shrapnel, feeding off of pain, misery, and hard drugs. Cursed to wander the Earth without the hope of death, it is reborn again and again to spread the gospel of hate, abuse, and genocide. But what if it's not the only monster out there? What if there's something worse? From Dave Brockie, the twisted genius behind GWAR, comes a novel about the darkest days of the twentieth century.

"Take the Long Way Home" Brian Keene - All across the world, people suddenly vanish in the blink of an eye. Gone. Steve, Charlie and Frank were just trying to get home when it happened. Trapped in the ultimate traffic jam, they watch as civilization collapses, claiming the souls of those around them. God has called his faithful home, but the invitations for Steve, Charlie and Frank got lost. Now they must set off on foot through a nightmarish post-apocalyptic landscape in search of answers. In search of God. In search of their loved ones. And in search of home.

"Baby's First Book of Seriously Fucked-Up Shit" Robert Devereaux - From an orgy between God, Satan, Adam and Eve to beauty pageants for fetuses. From a giant human-absorbing tongue to a place where God is in the eyes of the psychopathic. This is a party at the furthest limits of human decency and cruelty. Robert Devereaux is your host but watch out, he's spiked the punch with drugs, sex, and dismemberment. Deadite Press is proud to present nine stories of the strange, the gross, and the just plain fucked up.

THE VERY BEST IN CULT HORROR

deadite press

"Header" Edward Lee - In the dark backwoods, where law enforcement doesn't dare tread, there exists a special type of revenge. Something so awful that it is only whispered about. Something so terrible that few believe it is real. Stewart Cummings is a government agent whose life is going to Hell. His wife is ill and to pay for her medication he turns to bootlegging. But things will get much worse when bodies begin showing up in his sleepy small town. Victims of an act known only as "a Header."

"Red Sky" Nate Southard - When a bank job goes horrifically wrong, career criminal Danny Black leads his crew from El Paso into the deserts of New Mexico in a desperate bid for escape. Danny soon finds himself with no choice but to hole up in an abandoned factory, the former home of Red Sky Manufacturing. Danny and his crew aren't the only living things in Red Sky, though. Something waits in the abandoned factory's shadows, something horrible and violent. Something hungry. And when the sun drops, it will feast.

"Zombies and Shit" Carlton Mellick III - Twenty people wake to find themselves in a boarded-up building in the middle of the zombie wasteland. They soon discover they have been chosen as contestants on a popular reality show called Zombie Survival. Each contestant is given a backpack of supplies and a unique weapon. Their goal: be the first to make it through the zombie-plagued city to the pick-up zone alive. But because there's only one seat available on the helicopter, the contestants not only have to fight against the hordes of the living dead, they must also fight each other.

"All You Can Eat" Shane McKenzie - Deep in Texas there is a Chinese restaurant that harbors a secret. Its food is delicious and the secret ingredient ensures that once you have one bite you'll never be able to stop. But when the food runs out and the customers turn to cannibalism, the kitchen staff must take up arms against these obese people-eaters or else be next on the menu!

www.ingramcontent.com/pod-product-compliance
Lightning Source LLC
Chambersburg PA
CBHW051655260626
47170CB00004B/1508